INN FOR MURDER

A Wildflower Inn Mystery Book 1

HARPER LIN

This is a work of fiction. Names, characters, organizations, places, events, and incidents are either products of the author's imagination or are used fictitiously.

INN FOR MURDER

www.harperlin.com

Chapter 1

I had only been working at the Wildflower Inn for three days when I walked into the restaurant to find a dead body sprawled out on the floor. As the new reservation manager, my job was to ensure guests were satisfied, but here I was, standing in shock over a corpse, wondering what on earth had happened to upset a guest this much.

The restaurant, empty during mid-afternoon, was located in the basement of the inn, a stone mill heritage estate. When the candles were lit and the mood lighting turned on, it transformed into a romantic space. But even before I discovered the body, I couldn't ignore the strange new atmosphere that permeated the room—a cellar, really. The air was heavy with a sense of unease, as if the walls themselves were harboring some terrible secret.

I had been walking over to the comfortable leather couch facing the unlit fireplace, where guests usually gathered for cocktails and socializing before dinner. Though my break was only twenty minutes, I figured a quick catnap on the gingham cushions would be worth it since I'd been up so early. That's when I nearly stumbled over what, at first glance, looked like two giant sacks of potatoes.

My gaze fell to the floor. I screamed and staggered back. It was practically soundproof down there; I was sure no one could hear me. Lying on the floor was a body, eyes still wide open and unfocused. He wore a crisp-looking white linen suit and a pale blue dress shirt. No wounds were visible, but the way his body lay showed all too clearly that he was no longer alive.

I immediately recognized him. Caleb McAllister, an elderly white-haired man with deep-set wrinkles along his tanned face. He had just checked in at the inn yesterday.

My panic escalated as I tried to make sense of what had happened. I knew it was best to immediately leave and find help, but my curiosity took hold, and I couldn't resist taking a closer look at the body.

That's when I noticed something odd: clenched in Caleb's fingers was a piece of paper. It could have been a suicide note or something explaining his death—whatever it was, it seemed important enough for him to keep it with him until the very end.

I carefully grabbed the top of the paper with the tips of my fingers and pried it free. On one side was a drawing in bluepoint pen, some weird doodle containing a series of lines and two circles. When I turned the note around, I gasped. The handwriting was shaky, but I could make out the message: "Beware of the Amandes," it said.

My heart dropped. I had met the inn's owners, the Amandes family, just two weeks before. Stella Amandes was the matriarch of the family. Mostly retired, she still puttered around doing odd jobs. She was the one who had hired me. I'd also met her two sons, both around my age. Both handsome. Max was the inn's general manager, officially my boss, while Jesse was one of the inn's two cooks.

Max had chiseled features and dark brown hair that he kept neatly styled. He had a brooding demeanor and a commanding presence. On the few occasions I witnessed it, his charming smile could light up a room. Despite his position as my boss, he was approachable, always ready to lend a helping hand.

Jesse had a more laid-back demeanor. Sandy blond hair fell messily over his forehead, and a mischievous twinkle filled his blue eyes. He was always cracking jokes and making the kitchen staff laugh. But beneath his carefree exterior, there was a sharp intelligence and a determination to make the restaurant the best it could be.

I had noticed that the Amandes family had a certain allure that seemed to capture the attention of everyone they came into contact with. They were sophisticated yet friendly, but I also detected something mysterious beneath their polished exterior.

As I stood there, holding the note in my hand, I couldn't help but wonder what it meant. Did the Amandes family have something to do with Caleb's death? Or was someone else involved?

I knew I couldn't stand around contemplating the situation for much longer. I had to alert the police about the body. I quickly ran to the back office and grabbed the phone, dialing 911 with shaking fingers.

As I waited for the operator to pick up, my mind raced with other possible suspects. Was it a jealous ex-lover of Caleb? Or a business rival with a grudge? Perhaps another guest at the inn? I didn't know the man at all, and the possibilities seemed endless.

After several rings, an operator finally answered. I stuttered my way through the explanation, pausing every few words to collect my thoughts and steady my breath. I quickly relayed the awful situation: a body, a crime scene, the location. The operator offered reassurance that help was coming soon and warned me not to touch anything. Too late for that, I thought.

Finally, I hung up the phone and exhaled deeply, attempting to relieve just a fraction of the tension tightening my body. As I turned around, though, it felt like all the air had been sucked out of the room. Standing directly before me was Max—silent, still, ominously looming over me. He seemed frozen in time, watching me with those dark blue eyes.

"What's going on?" Max asked.

I hesitated for a moment, unsure of how much to reveal. But I knew I needed to tell him. "There's been a death," I said, my voice barely above a whisper.

Max's eyes widened in shock. "What kind of death?"

I swallowed hard, feeling a lump form in my throat. "A guest," I said. "Downstairs in the restaurant."

"What? Who?" he demanded.

"It's Caleb McAllister," I said, studying Max's reaction.

"Caleb? The new guest?"

"I found him just a few minutes ago," I said. "The police are on their way."

I continued watching him carefully. I wondered if I should tell him about the note, but I decided not to. It was best to wait for the police before I started speculating.

Max's jaw clenched as he processed the news. "I'll call Jesse and get him to round up the kitchen staff and keep them out of the restaurant," he said, his voice firm. "We don't want to contaminate the crime scene."

I nodded, grateful for his quick thinking. "I'll tell any staff I see. Stella too if she's back from town."

Max stood before the stairs leading down to the

restaurant to block it until the police came. It was fortunate that most guests were out and about this time of day.

The police arrived with sirens blaring. So much for discretion. I went outside to receive them.

Chapter 2

As the detective stepped out of the car and approached me, I couldn't help but feel a flutter in my stomach.

Detective J.T. Connor had a commanding presence that set him apart from the other officers. Tall and broad-shouldered, he towered over most people. He had a strong jawline, and wavy jet-black hair that was neatly combed and gelled. His well-tailored suit hugged his muscular frame, adding to his imposing presence. A small scar ran above his left eyebrow, a testament to years of experience on the force. His intense green eyes seemed to miss nothing.

He flashed me a brief smile that didn't quite reach his eyes.

"Do you work here?"

I nodded and introduced myself as Sophie, explaining that I was the one who had called. The police officer beside him scribbled it down in a small notepad. I tried to ignore the wave of dread that washed over me as I explained again what had happened: how I had found the dead guest with a note on him. I added a little fib, saying that I initially thought it had been a suicide note, so I'd picked it up to read it before leaving it beside him. I left out the detail about prying the note out of the dead man's clutch.

Detective Connor's gaze felt like needles on my skin as he pressed for more details, but somehow I managed to keep my composure and answer his questions. Afterward, I couldn't help feeling guilty —had I really just tampered with evidence and lied about it?

Once he heard enough, Detective Connor went down to the basement with his team. Max was allowed to go down with them. I stayed with the detective's associate, the police officer taking notes, as he clarified the details I gave.

After I finished and the officer accompanied the group down in the restaurant, I waited in the lobby, not knowing what else to do but wait for the police to finish their investigation. I felt like I was in a detective novel.

The inn was occupied by a quiet stillness. It was a far cry from my first couple of days of work when laughter and conversation filled every corner, along with the smell of freshly baked bread wafting in from the kitchen.

The atmosphere now was intense, and my brain couldn't stop spinning with questions. What if I got fired because of this situation? Even worse—what if I ended up a suspect in Caleb's murder somehow? Did it look bad that I stayed to read the note, leaving behind my fingerprints on the paper? Not to mention how guilty I felt for potentially ruining the police's chances of finding the set of fingerprints belonging to the real killer.

But then again, why would Caleb's killer give him a note warning him to be careful of the Amandes?

I concluded that the note was unlikely from the killer. Maybe the killer wanted the note and struggled to get it. It was all so mysterious.

After a while, several men in blue latex gloves came upstairs with Caleb's body in a black bag, then loaded it into the back of an ambulance that had come without the fanfare of sirens.

When the police officers finished their work hours later, the detective gave me a quick nod of acknowledgment. I smiled back weakly. Max came to me looking bewildered.

"The Wildflower Inn is shutting down," he told me.

"What?"

He quickly clarified. "Only temporarily, of course. Until the police finish their investigation," he said, his voice low. "They think Caleb might have been choked to death, but they have to confirm it with some tests. But this inn is officially a crime scene."

"But what about the guests? Do we ask them to leave?"

"The police are going to do background checks on all of them, but for now, they're going to have to find another inn to stay in. The restaurant will be closed, and we won't be checking in any more guests. We'll have to start calling any guests coming in this week and help them connect with one of the other inns in town too."

I nodded, feeling the weight of the situation beginning to settle in. "What about us? Are we suspects?"

"No," Max said firmly. "We all have alibis. We

weren't downstairs when it happened, so there's no reason to think we were involved in any way." He paused for a moment before continuing. "But like I said, the police might want to talk to us if they need more information."

I nodded, feeling a little reassured. But there was still the matter of that note, a warning about the Amandes. I bit my lip.

Max looked thoughtful. "We'll have to be tactful about this with guests. We don't want to cause any unnecessary panic."

I nodded again, feeling a little overwhelmed by the situation.

"It's okay," he said. "We can keep working on what we can do to get the guests sorted while we try not to think about it too much."

It being the murder.

Easier said than done, I thought. The Wildflower Inn had always been a peaceful, tranquil place, but now it felt like a dark cloud had descended upon it.

Jesse came running in the front door. He was carrying a bag of groceries. He still hadn't changed into his chef's uniform yet and was wearing his usual James Dean-ish ensemble of blue jeans and a white T-shirt.

"I saw all the police cars on the road and an ambulance. What happened?"

Max made hand gestures to keep his voice low. He calmly explained what had happened and how I had discovered the body. Then he shared the details of what the police had said.

Jesse dropped the groceries and came over to me. He placed a comforting hand on my shoulder.

"Hey," he murmured softly. "You look shaken. Are you okay?"

"It's unbelievable...I just don't understand what happened."

He pulled me into an embrace and whispered calmingly in my ear. "It'll be okay." When he stood back, he shook his head. "It's only your third day on the job, right? I promise, this is not something that happens often."

I looked over Jesse's shoulder and saw Max with his arms crossed over his chest. He was staring at us with a hard expression, as if he was not impressed with the display of affection. For a moment, I thought he was going to say something, but he didn't. Instead, he turned and walked out of the lobby, past the reception, out into the back gardens.

Chapter 3

As evening rolled around, I found myself sitting alone in my room, unable to shake the sense of unease that had settled over the inn. Stella was graciously allowing me to stay in an unoccupied guest room until I found my own apartment. Having moved to Sierra Hills right after landing the job, I was still familiarizing myself with the town.

Perched by the window, gazing out at the vineyards behind the inn, I felt a sense of awe at the natural beauty of the place. It was very different from where I lived before, in a bustling city that never slept, where streets were perpetually filled with people, while buildings towered over them.

Sierra Hills, on the other hand, was a quaint

town known for its vineyards and charming architecture. Life moved at a slower pace here, with rolling hills, rows of grapevines stretching into the distance, fresh air, and streets lined with cozy shops and quaint cafes. The people here were always friendly and welcoming, creating a genuine sense of community that I had never experienced before. From farmers' markets to local festivals, there was always something going on. The Wildflower Inn stood at the heart of it all, and I felt privileged to be a part of it. Sierra Hills was a popular tourist destination, particularly during the harvest season when the vineyards were at their peak. It was a place where people came to relax, unwind, and revel in the simple pleasures of life. Despite my short time here, it already felt like home.

However, with the murder investigation casting a shadow over everything, the feeling of comfort and safety had been replaced with danger and suspicion. Lying in bed, staring at the ceiling, I wondered what the future held for me and for Sierra Hills. Would the inn ever regain its former charm, or would the memory of the murder always overshadow it?

Despite the uneasiness, I couldn't deny the town's beauty and charm. As I looked out the window, the sun setting over the vineyards cast a warm orange glow over everything.

My thoughts drifted to my ex-boyfriend, Ansel. The breakup was still fresh. We had met at my old job working at a four-star hotel in the city. For the first four months, we had been inseparable. At first, everything had been perfect. We shared similar interests and dreams. I fell in love fast.

Gradually, things started to change. Ansel became more possessive and controlling. He disapproved of my relationships with friends and colleagues. He often checked my phone, scrutinized my emails, and reprimanded me for going out without him, even on simple errands. Attempts to talk and reason with him always ended in fights. Although I tried to leave him once, he begged me to come back, promising to change. For a while, he did change, but eventually, he slipped back into his old ways.

The breaking point came when I caught him kissing a new coworker in the break room. Devastated but also relieved, I took the opportunity to move out of the tiny apartment we shared and break up with him for good. Nevertheless, Ansel wouldn't leave me alone. I was bombarded with constant calls, texts, unannounced visits to my friend's apartment where I was temporarily staying. He even followed me sometimes to my new job at a competing hotel.

After some struggle, I managed to get a restraining order to keep Ansel away from me. However, the emotional scars ran deep. Trust and insecurity lingered when it came to men, even though I had moved five states away from him.

Ansel haunted my nightmares and sometimes in waking life like a threatening shadow in the corner of my eye that disappeared whenever I tried to discern its shape.

Shaking my head to clear my troubled thoughts, I reaffirmed to myself that Ansel belonged to the past.

Sierra Hills represented my future.

Determined to create a new life without controlling ex-boyfriends or restraining orders, I stood up. I wanted some fresh air. Maybe a stroll in the gardens would do me good.

As soon as I walked outside, a rush of air brushed against my skin. I took a deep breath. The smell of roses filled the atmosphere, providing a tranquil contrast to the day's chaotic events. My steps echoed softly on the cobblestone path as I also admired the hydrangeas and daisies lining my way.

Suddenly, a sharp noise coming from the bushes made me freeze in place. My heart pounded.

Was it an intruder? Caleb's killer?

Fear tingled across my skin. I let out a gasp when I saw a figure coming towards me.

But a wave of relief washed over me when I recognized it was Max. Clutching a mystery novel, he walked toward me with a smile. He was likely heading to one of the benches where I'd seen him read before.

"Hey," he said. "Did I scare you?"

"No." I blushed, embarrassed.

"It's getting dark. Maybe you shouldn't be out here, with, you know…"

"The killer." I nodded. "I know. I just needed some air."

"How are you holding up?"

"I wish we could do something about it." I sighed. "Help the police somehow."

"They've finished questioning all the guests, and all we can do is give them access to the place so they can do their jobs."

I turned around and looked at the now-empty inn. All the windows of the rooms were dark.

"Poor Caleb. Did you manage to find his family?" I asked.

"I don't have that information, unfortunately, but the police said they would handle that too."

I felt sick at the thought of how Caleb's wife or children, if he had any, would feel receiving that phone call.

Max and I stood in silence for a moment, gazing out at the gardens, then at each other. A strange flutter gripped my stomach, a mix of nerves and excitement. I wondered if Max felt it too.

Max's gaze held intensity, a newfound openness.

"You know," he said, breaking the silence, "when I first got here, I thought this place would be boring. But now... now I can't imagine ever leaving. I feel like something special drew me here."

I smiled in agreement. "Yeah, there's definitely something about this place that's hard to explain."

"Hey, Sophie," he said softly. "Can I ask you something?"

"Sure."

"Why did you choose Sierra Hills?" he asked.

I hesitated, wanted to avoid revealing too much about my past.

"I just needed a change of scenery, and Sierra Hills seemed like the perfect place to start fresh."

It was the truth.

"I understand the need for a fresh start. That's

why my family and I decided to buy the vineyard," Max shared. "We've always been in the wine indus- try, and we were looking for a change. After my father passed away, we decided to leave the old vineyard to my uncle, let him restructure the busi- ness. We wanted to build something from the ground up and be a part of a new community. Sierra Hills just felt right."

"I'm sorry to hear about your dad." I offered comfort with a hand on his shoulder.

He smiled sadly, clearing his throat. "Thanks."

"I hope we can make the inn a better place," I said. "For the whole community, not just the tourists."

"I think we can," Max declared, his voice low. "Together."

Chapter 4

I woke up just as the sun began to tint the room with its first golden rays. With a soft yawn, I sat up, absorbing the coziness of my surroundings that I wasn't quite used to yet.

The room, though small, was decorated in a cottage style. Next to my vintage vanity table was a trio of photographs in different antique frames on a wall. On one of my nightstands sat a vase brimming with freshly picked wildflowers. Surely that was the handiwork of Stella. The cream floral wallpaper and green shiplap cemented the cozy cottage ambiance.

For a moment, yesterday's events felt like a nightmare. Then reality rushed back to me as I threw off my covers and prepared for the day. I had to face the living nightmare of what happened in the restaurant—finding Caleb's lifeless body, and the unsettling, mysterious note left behind.

A chill ran down my spine at the memory of the ominous message: "Be careful of the Amandes" and the peculiar drawing on the other side of the paper. The police now had that note. Could I trust them to get to the bottom of it?

Detective Connor had shown competence throughout this investigation. He and his team had stayed late into the evening. Jesse offered to cook them dinner, but they gracefully declined to maintain their professionalism.

I wondered if Detective Connor secretly suspected the Amandes due to the note. While he was likely to pursue other leads, the shadow of suspicion loomed over everyone, including myself. Max and Jesse didn't know about the note; I hadn't shared it with them. Did I suspect them too? Despite their unwavering kindness, I couldn't rule them out.

Before I could dress for the day, my gaze was drawn to the framed photos on the wall. When the Amandes bought the inn, they decided to keep all the original decor. They likely had little or no knowledge of the people captured in those photographs. Yet, I found myself staring intently at the images.

The main photograph showcased a beautiful family of six, standing in front of the inn. It looked like it was taken in the '60s. The parents, in their thirties, radiated warmth, the father's arm around the mother's waist, both holding a child's hand. Complementary outfits adorned the four kids—two boys in white shirts and dark pants, and two girls in matching flowy dresses with delicate lace edging.

The second photo captured the same family, now grown, sharing laughter around a table in what seemed like the '80s. There were plates piled high with food, and wine bottles scattered across the table. The father, now older, had his arm around the mother, and all the adult children looked happy and content.

The third, a detailed close-up of the two eldest kids, at a more recent cadence, revealing the aging process. It must have been taken fifteen, twenty years ago. They sat on one of the benches in the inn's garden, probably the spot Max favored for reading.

In the photograph, the man, deep in middle age, sported graying hair and wore a linen suit. His smile seemed friendly, yet a hint of melancholy lingered in his eyes, suggesting a deeper sadness. The lady beside him appeared plain and stern, her white sundress reminiscent of her childhood innocence, but that didn't extend to her expression, which was now weathered and weary.

The photographs drew me in, sparking curiosity about the family's story. Were any of them still alive? Some, now in their twilight years, might still be around. Could they have been the ones who sold the inn to the Amandes?

I ran my fingertips along the glass, tracing the grainy details of the smiling faces from the first photograph. Exhaling, I finally tore my eyes away and stumbled towards my bedroom closet.

There was no urgency in getting ready for work. Yesterday, I had made all the necessary calls, informing guests of the inn's sudden closure due to an emergency. Surprisingly understanding, they found accommodations in competing inns in town. Now, here I was, with nothing else to do since no one was coming.

I could try to find out more about Caleb, even

though he had come alone. While I doubted the other staff knew much, it wouldn't hurt to ask.

If Lucinda Foreman was around, I could also ask her about the previous owners of the inn. She had worked as the vineyard manager here for over thirty years. Lucinda would surely know more about the inn and its history than anyone else.

Chapter 5

I spotted Lucinda in the inn when I went into the breakfast and lunch restaurant on the ground floor. Lucinda was a tall woman around sixty with shoulder-length gray hair she usually tied in a low ponytail so she could wear her sunhat when she worked under the sun. Her deep, melodic voice exuded authority, and in the few times I've seen her around, I was impressed with the graceful way she led her team in the vineyards.

After finishing her cup of coffee, she placed it on the tray for used dishes, and looked ready to start her work. As she turned to leave, she noticed me approaching and gave me a warm welcome.

"Good morning, dear. How are you doing?"

"It could be better," I replied.

"You don't say. That was quite the day yesterday. Did you sleep well?"

"I did," I said. "My room's really nice. Very cozy decor. There are some photographs in there. Have you seen them?"

"Perhaps. What do they look like?" she asked.

I described the photographs in my room of the big family and casually asked if she knew them.

Lucinda listened intently and then nodded. "Ah, I know who you're talking about. That's the Reynolds family. They founded the inn."

"Really? What happened to them?" I asked.

Lucinda's face clouded over. "It's a sad story, dear. The Reynolds family was very close, and this inn had been in the family since the kids were young. It used to be profitable enough. When both the parents passed away, the eldest kids, Beatrice and Stephen, ended up running the place. They didn't always see eye to eye, and they ended up in some financial troubles. They had to sell the inn ten years ago to pay off some debts. Then the Byrons had been running this inn and vineyard for the past decade. They were the ones responsible for the renovations and interior design of the guest rooms too. They came with money, which helped. They kept some photographs of the Reynolds as part of the decor to respect the heritage of this place."

"What happened to the Reynolds family?" I asked.

"I'm sure they paid off whatever debt was owed with the sale of this place, and they're probably retired somewhere."

"Interesting. Thanks. I've been curious about the history of this place."

"You're welcome, dear. Even though this inn is only around 60 years old, it's still nice to learn."

I nodded, wondering if I should ask her about the murder. I decided to go ahead, having nothing to lose. "Did the police question you yesterday too?"

Lucinda nodded grimly. "Yes, they did. I told them everything I knew, but I don't think I was much help. I didn't see or hear anything out of the ordinary yesterday since I was out working in the vineyards with my crew."

"Do you think there's anything peculiar about any of the guests?" I asked.

Lucinda chuckled. "I've been working here for three decades, dear. I've seen all kinds of guests come and go. But I don't recall anything unusual about any of the guests we've had recently. Did you?"

"Not really," I said. "We're lucky we only had five other guests yesterday."

"Tuesdays are slow sometimes." Lucinda nodded.

"Did you ever see Caleb, the guest who, you know, passed away?"

"I must've seen him, but sometimes I get so distracted with work that I don't notice. I don't recall talking to him though. I'm sure he didn't deserve to die the way he did."

We talked a bit more about what happened yesterday, then I let Lucinda get to work.

I went to look at my breakfast options. The usual buffet-style spread for the guests was gone. Not even toast was out. No wonder Lucinda was only drinking coffee. Luckily, Jesse popped out. He wore an apron over his white T-shirt.

"Good morning, miss. What can I make for you?" he asked with a friendly wink. "I make a mean omelette."

"Oh, is the kitchen still open? I was just going to get some cereal."

"The kitchen is open just for you."

"Okay." I couldn't help but grin back. "Scrambled eggs?"

"I can make you some scrambled eggs with home fries and toast if you like."

"That sounds amazing, thank you."

As Jesse headed back into the kitchen, my thoughts returned to the Reynolds family and their history with the inn. What kind of debt could they have had that forced them to sell? Business seemed good now. Tourists flocked in droves to stay here, especially on the weekends. Weddings happened here all the time. Lucinda did mention something about the Byrons investing money in renovations. Maybe the inn wasn't in such great shape before.

Jesse came back with two plates, the scent of freshly cooked food filling the room. I was happy that he was eating with me. He settled into the seat across from me with a contented sigh.

"I love it when I get a chance to cook for someone," he said. "I miss the guests already. I really hope they catch the killer soon."

"I wish I could do more to help."

"I think you helped enough." I looked up at him with bewildered eyes.

"With finding Caleb and everything," Jesse clarified. "That must've been a shock."

I looked down at my plate. "Yeah."

"Let's talk about something else," he said. "I

don't want to spoil your appetite. Nothing we can do about it now except wait anyway."

"Okay." I squeezed some ketchup on my plate. "Have you met the previous owners of this inn?"

"Oh, the Byrons?" Jesse nodded as he took a bite of his eggs. "Yeah, I've met them a few times. They were nice people. A couple in their late fifties."

"Why did they sell?"

"They wanted to be near their kids and grand-kids on the East Coast, so they moved back. I guess they had some vague idea of retiring on a vineyard, but in the end, they realized they had to work more than they expected, and they knew they didn't want to work this hard once they actually got to retire-ment age."

I nodded and took a bite of my toast. I asked Jesse about the Reynolds family too, mentioning the photos in my room.

"The Reynolds family, huh? I've heard some stories about them. I never had any direct contact with them, but the Byrons had some stories."

"What kind of stories?" I asked, intrigued.

"Well, for starters, there was some tension between the siblings. Apparently, Beatrice wanted to sell the inn, and Stephen was against it. They were

both not great at business. They were hemor-
rhaging money at some point when Stephen wanted
to have these extravagant buffet lunches. Beatrice
wanted to cut their losses, but Stephen wanted to
keep trying. They fought about it a lot, and they
ultimately sold. I think they were forced to sell
because they were in debt. Sometimes the locals still
talk about them, but they don't live in town
anymore. I don't know what happened to them."

"I hope they're able to retire comfortably," I
said.

Jesse nodded. "Yeah, I hope so too. It's a shame.
The Reynolds family had owned the inn for
decades, and it was a staple of the community. But I
guess sometimes things just don't work out. It's not
always easy to be making wine and also running an
inn at the same time."

I made a mental note to do some more digging
and see if I could find out more about their financial troubles. It seemed like there were a lot of
secrets and tensions brewing beneath the surface of
this place. And now, with a murder happening at
the inn, it made me wonder if there was some sort
of connection between the past and the present.
But maybe I was just reaching.

"Did you know Caleb at all?" I asked Jesse.

He frowned. "Caleb? You mean the victim?"

I nodded.

"Not personally, but I've seen him around. I think he liked his eggs sunny side up. He was one of the guests who checked in a day ago, right? Seemed friendly enough."

"Did you see him talking to anyone else?" I asked.

Jesse shook his head. "No." He looked up at me, smiling. "You sound like the police. Are you going Nancy Drew on me?"

I shrugged, smiling. "I just feel responsible, since he was a guest and I was the one who found him."

"Don't blame yourself. You have nothing to do with it."

But can I keep working for you if your family does? I thought to myself, remembering the note.

Chapter 6

After breakfast, I decided to walk around the vineyard. The fresh air and tranquil surroundings helped to clear my mind. Although thoughts about Caleb lingered—how he was discovered in the restaurant when no one else was present. Did he expect the bar to be open so he could have a drink? Was he meeting someone there? Or did he, like me, simply want to be somewhere quiet?

I had the idea to go to Caleb's room, despite the police having already investigated and collected his belongings. I probably shouldn't. In fact, I really shouldn't.

But I was curious. Maybe I could just take a quick peek.

Back inside the inn, I took the set of master keys behind the counter, and I went up the stairs. The entire floor had an eerie silence.

Caleb's room mirrored any other, featuring a queen-sized bed, a dresser, a vanity table, and a view of the vineyards. Unlike my room, his lacked photographs of the Reynolds family. Instead, I found an oil painting of the town on the wall. I checked the nightstands and their drawers, where Caleb's belongings had been just yesterday. Now, they were all empty.

A wave of sorrow washed over me. This had been Caleb's home during his final days. I wondered if the person who took his life was someone he trusted, someone he willingly allowed into his room.

The inn's lack of security worried me. They lagged behind the times when it came to cameras and alarms. They didn't even have a smart door-bell. With no concrete evidence, it would be a challenge for the police to identify a potential killer among guests or staff. The realization sent shivers down my spine as I contemplated how easily someone could get away with murder inside this inn.

Finding nothing useful in the room, I came out

and locked the door behind me. As soon as I did, I heard footsteps coming up the staircase. They sounded too slow, too hesitant—they raised my suspicion.

I hid myself around the corner and waited. Whoever it was stopped in front of Caleb's door and unlocked it. I took a peek.

It was Marty, an old family friend of the Amandes. Retired like Stella, Marty often assisted with odd jobs around the inn, including fixing plumbing issues in the rooms. That explained his access to keys. But that didn't explain what he was doing inside Caleb's room.

I often found him sharing laughter with Stella while working in the gardens. I had wondered about Marty's connection with Stella, suspecting more than a casual friendship. Why else would he offer to work so much around the inn for free?

I waited before following him into the room, convinced his visit wasn't about plumbing. And I was right.

I found Marty, standing by the dresser, sifting through drawers. Clearing my throat made him jump in surprise.

"What are you doing here?" he asked, his face flushed with embarrassment.

"I could ask you the same thing," I replied, aiming for a non-threatening tone.

Marty hesitated. "I was just looking for something."

"Like what?"

"Something the police might have missed."

"The police cleared everything out yesterday," I informed him.

"Oh. I didn't know that." His nervousness was evident.

"Did you know the guest?" I asked.

"No," he answered too quickly. "Although I've said hi to him in passing."

"Did you notice anything suspicious that might help the police with their investigation?"

After a moment's contemplation, Marty said, "Actually yes. I overheard Caleb talking on his cell phone the night before he died. Down in the lobby."

"With whom?"

"I couldn't hear the other side of the conversation, but he mentioned going out for drinks with someone. That's why I came to look for clues. I had to try."

"Did you tell the police?"

"They didn't question me. I wasn't around."

"Well, they should know," I insisted.

Marty considered it. "You're right."

"I know it's awkward to talk to the police, but it's important. Whoever Caleb was meeting for drinks might be involved in his death."

"Of course," he said. "I'll go to the station right now."

Exiting the room, I extended my palm. After another moment's hesitation, he handed me the keys, looking somewhat ashamed.

"Just be careful, okay, miss?" he said. "We don't know who we're dealing with here."

Chapter 7

I passed Stella trimming the bushes in the gardens as I set off down a different path, making my way towards the gazebo. The air was filled with the harmonious hum of cicadas and a soft rustling of leaves stirred up by the wind.

My steps echoed through the gazebo as I stepped onto the wooden floorboards. A romantic feeling washed over me, and I closed my eyes, letting the gentle breeze play with my hair. When I opened them again, I saw Max in the distance walking towards me. His white dress shirt was untucked over jeans. I'd never seen him outside of his former work suits. His hair was tousled, as if he had just stepped out of bed, which only made him look even more irresistible.

"Hey," I said, pushing back the nerves bubbling up inside of me.

"Hey yourself," he said with a grin, making his way up the gazebo stairs to join me.

I couldn't help but notice the way his eyes roamed over my body for a quick moment. I felt a shiver run down my spine as he came up and closed the distance between us.

I thought about telling Max how I encountered Marty in Caleb's room, about how Marty overheard that phone call from Caleb. But I decided not to. I still didn't know whether I could trust Max or any of the Amandes. And I couldn't let my little crush on him get in the way of the facts. Max was still a suspect, to me anyway. The Amandes might still be connected with Caleb's death somehow. Until I knew more, I couldn't let Max know I was snooping around.

"We keep meeting like this," he said.

"Come around often?" I asked, trying to keep the conversation light.

Max leaned against a railing of the gazebo. "Honestly, I just needed to get away from the office for a bit."

"It's so relaxing out here." I felt awkward, not knowing what else to say.

Max's eyes locked onto mine. "When I'm here, it's like everything else fades away. It's just me, the sound of the wind, and the beauty of this place."

We both stood there, soaking in the tranquility of the garden and the company of each other. Again. Max placed his hand on my shoulder, his touch sending electricity down my spine. For a moment, I thought he was going to lean in and kiss me, but he stepped back.

"I wish I could go hiking today and take the whole day off," Max said, breaking the spell that had surrounded us. "But I have to stick around. The police are coming again."

I nodded, trying to keep the disappointment out of my voice. "Yeah, I'll be around if you need me."

Max said he would leave me to enjoy the gardens and that he had to prepare for the police to come. I sighed as I watched him walk away. I wondered what would have happened if he had kissed me. I shook my head, trying to clear my thoughts. I needed to focus on the case, not Max and his intoxicating presence.

As I stood in the gazebo, I thought about Caleb and who he had met for drinks. That person must've given him the note. And he or she must've known the Amandes too. But what was that drawing on the other side? Even though I had already given it to the police, I did remember what it looked like. A series of lines and two circles. What did it represent? What was Caleb doing in the restaurant cellar with that drawing? Alone. If I had gotten down there when he was alive, what would I find?

Seeing as all of the inn and restaurant staff weren't coming in, I figured I might as well take a chance and go down to the restaurant myself. Any evidence that might be found could help shed some light on why Caleb was murdered.

I put my hair up in a bun. In the kitchen, Jesse wasn't around, and I took a couple of disposable rubber gloves. I slipped them on so as not to mess anything up. I went down the stairwell that led to the restaurant, ready to explore. But I had to be quick before the police came.

Once inside the basement, I flipped the light switch on and inspected the restaurant. It was almost exactly like how I'd previously seen it – minus the corpse. As I looked around, I noticed some of the furniture had been moved, but nothing seemed out of place.

I wondered what I was supposed to find. I swept the room once, twice, searching for any clues that could shed light on Caleb's mysterious death. My eyes landed on a bookshelf tucked away in one corner of the cellar. It was a small shelf full of the crime novels Max liked so much, but what caught my attention were the two lights mounted on the wall above it. They were in the same position and shape as the two circles in the drawing.

Chapter 8

I felt a chill rush through my body as the realization hit me. Was this just a stroke of luck? My pulse quickened, and I slowly walked towards the wall, inspecting every detail of the lights with eagerness.

The round lights looked more decorative than functional. In the short time I'd been here, I'd never seen them turned on. But each of them had a small button underneath, barely perceptible. I pressed one. It didn't turn on. I pressed the other light's button. That didn't turn on either. I tried the first one again. Nothing.

I stepped back and looked at it. I turned around to leave, but as I took a step back, the bookcase opened a crack towards me like a door.

A hidden room?

My stomach churned with fear. I was terrified. What if this was the place where the murderer had been hiding?

I hesitated for a moment, but my curiosity eventually got the best of me, and I pushed the bookshelf open with my gloved hands. The "door" creaked and groaned loudly as it opened up into a dark abyss. I was petrified and wondered if I should even proceed. But something inside me told me that I should take a step into the unknown if I wanted to solve Caleb's murder.

Taking a deep breath to calm my nerves, I decided to go for it.

I switched on the flashlight app of my phone. I swung the door open. In an instant, the contents of the room were revealed; a single bare lightbulb swayed from its wire above me. I found the light switch. With a click, the room was illuminated in its entirety.

It was almost too incredible to believe. I had found what appeared to be a hidden wine cellar, filled with ancient wine. There were rows and rows of bottles, some on racks and some sitting on shelves, musty and coated with a thin layer of dust.

I slowly walked through the aisles of glass

bottles, gazing upon each one in awe. These were no ordinary wines – all vintage and rare. This was like stumbling upon a treasure trove.

I recognized a bottle of 1961 Chateau Margaux. Was this the wine that was worth thousands? The label was worn and faded, but I could still make out the distinctive emblem of the chateau. It looked authentic.

But then I noticed the cork. It seemed to be crumbling and dry, with little bits of it floating inside the dark wine. That wouldn't bode well for its taste or integrity.

I tried another bottle, a 1945 Romanee-Conti, with a pristine label and a wax seal over the cork. And many more expensive vintage wines.

As I continued to explore the hidden wine cellar, I noticed a small workshop space tucked away in the corner. I cautiously walked towards it, not wanting to disturb anything.

A large wooden table was cluttered with various tools and equipment. There were rows of test tubes, beakers, and flasks, along with a large machine that resembled a distiller.

It dawned on me what this was. Someone had been duplicating these rare and expensive vintage wines and selling them as the real thing.

I looked around the room, trying to find any evidence that could lead me to the culprit. That's when I noticed a small notebook lying on the table. I carefully flipped through it, which confirmed what I suspected. It contained detailed notes on the creation of each fake wine, including the types of grapes used, the aging process, and even the temperature and humidity conditions required to duplicate the perfect vintage, not to mention the aroma and notes of each wine, color of the original bottle, as well as other intricate instructions.

Who would go to such lengths to create fake wine? And who would be buying this fake wine? If someone was going to the trouble of producing it, there had to be a demand for it. Caleb must have uncovered this workshop and its illegal activities, and that could explain why he was killed.

This place seemed old and unused for years, so it couldn't have been the Amandes. Was it the Byrons or the Reynolds?

I took out my phone and took a few photos of the wine racks, the duplication system, some pages of the book. Then I came out of the secret room and closed the bookcase door behind me.

Anxiously, I surveyed my surroundings, making sure I was still the only one in the restaurant. My heart raced as I looked at the clock on one wall. It wouldn't be long before the police arrived. I had to get out of here or risk being caught.

Only I knew about this hidden room. Should I tell Max? Jesse? Stella? Marty?

No. I should only tell Detective Connor. He was the only person I could trust so far. I just had to get him alone to do so.

When I went into the breakfast area, Jesse and Stella were already there, talking quietly to each other. I quickly took off my gloves and stuffed them in the back pockets of my jeans. Stella was a striking woman in her sixties. Despite her years, she had an almost ethereal beauty, with high cheekbones, piercing blue eyes, and a cascade of snowy white hair that fell in soft waves around her face.

She hugged me and asked me how I'd slept. We made small talk, and I tried to keep up my pleasant demeanor to cover up the shock of my discovery.

Jesse offered me coffee with his usual easygoing grin. I politely declined and thanked him. Max joined us. As I looked between the two brothers, I felt a twinge of guilt. They had been so kind to me, and I was still suspecting them, and keeping important information about their property from them.

But I was going to tell the detective, and he

would tell them soon enough. I walked to the front entrance and looked out the window.

Soon two cars arrived, one a police cruiser, and another an incognito black car.

Detective Connor stepped out of the black car looking handsome in his pressed suit and navy tie. I noticed there was no ring on his finger. I wondered why he was single, before quickly reminding myself it wasn't the time or place to ogle men. He strode towards the door, his gaze meeting mine through the pane of glass with an intensity that could be read from a mile away.

I rushed out the door and greeted him, telling him there was something I wanted to speak to him about in private, quickly, away from my bosses. He looked at me with a quizzical frown. But he agreed as we moved away from the windows and under some trees where there was more foliage and fewer prying eyes. I couldn't help but think that this might have been an incredibly romantic spot for any other time. Had I been too single and dateless for too long? I groaned inwardly at myself.

I leaned in as I began to explain. Smelling his cologne was a bonus. "You know that note Caleb McAllister had? It turns out, it was a map."

Detective Connor's eyes narrowed with curiosity. He crossed his arms and replied, "Oh really? How do you know this?"

"Because I found a hidden cellar," I said.

Chapter 9

My heart pounded like a raw steak being tenderized by a mallet as I watched Detective Connor and his team descending into the restaurant. He had promised to keep the hidden room a secret while conducting his murder investigation, acting as if he stumbled upon it himself. His stoic demeanor didn't reveal much, but I trusted him.

I sat back at the kitchen table with the Amandes. Stella, Max, and Jesse all wore somber expressions filled with tension. Their silence and stillness made them seem like statues. To break the oppressive atmosphere, I tried to make conversation.

"You know, I really miss seeing new faces around here," I said.

"I can't believe it was only last week that we had that wedding for that couple from Texas," Jesse said.

"The food was really something, wasn't it?" I said with a grin. "I mean, those lobster rolls are still stuck in my mind. Delicious!"

Jesse grinned in response. "That's the first time I made them, on the bride's request. I think I'll work them into the lunch menu at some point."

I noticed Max frowning slightly as he looked between us.

"Fingers crossed we'll be open again by the weekend," I said.

"We'll have to know soon," Max said. "If we don't get the go-ahead to reopen by tonight or tomorrow at the earliest, we'll have to keep sending guests to the other inns."

Max looked at me with concern etched on his face. I knew what he was thinking. The guests weren't coming, but the staff still needed to be paid. I didn't know much about the Amandes' finances, but it couldn't be good for business to have murder disrupt it. We had two more weddings booked later this month.

It didn't take a genius to realize that murder at their business would hurt their finances and possibly ruin them if news got out about Caleb's death. He was only a tourist to the town. No one seemed to know him in Sierra Hills, and there was no indication of gossip or news reports so far. Which was good for us. But it was a small town. News could spread.

"I've been thinking," Stella chimed in. "If worse comes to worst, maybe we can offer some sort of deal to attract guests back."

Max nodded in agreement, "That's a good idea. Maybe like a two-night stay for the price of one or something like that."

"We can collaborate with the local spa," I suggested. "We can work with their masseuses and offer some sort of weekend pampering package."

"That's a great idea," Jesse said. "We'll advertise it on our website and social media pages."

But Max's face darkened. "As long as there's a killer still around, I can't exactly feel good about guests being back so soon."

I wanted to comfort him with a hug and tell him that everything was going to be alright, but I held myself back. I did the professional thing and offered a sympathetic look.

Part of me yearned to be part of the action downstairs, though I knew it was for my own good to keep a low profile in this discovery. Anxiously, I fidgeted with the linen tablecloth, then consciously placed my hands on my lap to avoid further rustling of the fabric.

By lunchtime, Detective Connor finally emerged from the restaurant. From the way he looked at me, lingering for a beat too long, I knew he had followed my instructions, and now, his team was down there exploring the mysterious wine cellar accessed through the trap door. He had pushed the first button beneath the left light of the bookcase, then the second beneath the light on the right, and the first one again to open it. I wondered what else they had uncovered beyond what I had already seen.

I held my breath as I waited for him to give me a sign. Of course, I knew he was consciously sealing himself off from me, but I wanted so badly to ask him.

"I need to ask you all something," the detective said, his gaze shifting from Stella, Max, and Jesse, and back to me. He stood over the table, looming in a stance of domination. My palms started to sweat, as if I had done something wrong.

Stella cleared her throat before she spoke. "Of course Detective. What do you need?"

"Did you know about the wine cellar?"

"Yes, of course, we have hundreds of bottles down there."

"No, not the one you already use as a stock room. The secret one behind the bookcase."

Max and Jesse exchanged a glance of utter amazement, their eyes widening in surprise. Stella's mouth fell agape. I watched them carefully, and it was clear that their shock was genuine.

Detective Connor went on to explain the hidden cellar, and how he and his team were able to unlock it thanks to a diagram found on Caleb's person. Despite his professional demeanor, it was clear that he was excited about this particular discovery, just as I had been.

"This is totally insane," Jesse exclaimed. "It's like something straight out of an *Indiana Jones* movie!"

Stella slowly shook her head in disbelief, "I had no idea that was down here."

"The bookcase was the door all this time?" Max asked.

Detective Connors nodded. "So none of you knew?"

"No," they all said.

"Do you think any of your other employees would know about it?"

"We're new owners," Max said. "We're still getting familiar with the ins and outs of this property, but some of our staff have been working here for decades. Lucina, our vineyard manager, has been working here the longest."

"I will be questioning her and everyone else on staff again," Detective Connor said, looking at everyone, including me, searchingly. I could tell he believed the Amandes. They were not suspects. They were new in town, just as I was. I breathed a sigh of relief.

"Can we see the cellar?" Jesse asked, sounding excited. "I mean, after your team finishes in there?"

"It's still a crime scene," Detective Connor said. "Everything is evidence, and the space is off-limits for now."

Jesse looked disappointed.

"What's in that wine cellar?" Max asked. "What was Caleb looking for?"

Detective Connor exhaled slowly; he seemed a little uneasy. Instead of sharing his suspicion of the wine forgery, all he said was, "We're still working out what happened here. If there's anything I need to know, I'll ask."

"Whoever didn't want Caleb into that secret cellar was the killer,"Max said.

The detective looked reluctant to respond, but he gave a slow nod. "This is why it's imperative to talk to everyone on your staff. Someone in this inn might know about the secret cellar."

"I can't imagine someone on our staff being the killer." Stella shook her head, not wanting to believe it. I knew she already thought of the staff as family. I did too. Wanted to, anyway.

Max gave Detective Connor instructions on how to find Lucinda in the vineyards. I wondered if Lucinda really did know anything about the secret wine cellar.

Lucinda was a wine expert. Could her extensive knowledge and years of experience have been used for something more sinister? Was it possible she had used it to fake rare varieties to be passed off as the real expensive stuff? I tried not to jump to conclusions, and she seemed like a friendly, pleasant woman. But what did I truly know about Lucinda anyway?

When I was down there, the cellar had looked a little dusty, and no one had been in there for a while. I wondered when was the last time someone had been in there trying to forge a bottle. If

Lucinda was the forger, she would've been down there working recently.

Unless the operation had been shut down long ago because whoever was involved didn't want to get into trouble. Could Lucinda have killed Caleb because he was poking his nose where he didn't belong? Did she kill him so she wouldn't be implicated in the crime ring?

It was out of my hands now. Detective Connor would get to the bottom of it.

He seemed open to my help. I hadn't gotten into trouble yet, even though I shouldn't have touched that note. He didn't even reprimand me for being down in the restaurant when it was a crime scene. If I hadn't looked at that piece of paper or went back into the restaurant yesterday, I wouldn't have found the secret cellar.

Maybe I could be of more use. But how? I had to balance being respectful of Detective Connor's process and helping. I would just have to keep my eyes and ears open.

I decided to stick around the inn in case Detective Connor wanted to find me. I took up Stella's offer to pick wildflowers in the garden. Aside from the wine, it was what the inn was known for, hence the name. She handed me one of her baskets, and we started picking. It was fun and relaxing. I could see why she did this all the time.

Stella created bouquets for the guest rooms, two restaurants in town, and even made an exquisite wedding bouquet for the last bride. But with no idea when guests would return, these beautiful creations might sit unappreciated around the inn.

Jesse, having no other guests to cook for lunch, came out to chat with us in the garden as we worked.

"An oven-roasted lemon and herb chicken was on the guest menu for today," he said. "It's a new recipe that I had tweaked into my own."

He loved cooking for people, seeing their delight as they took the first few bites.

"I'm sure you'll be able to make it soon," I said.

He shrugged. "I take comfort in schedules, but what can I do? Life is unpredictable."

"Are you bored, son?" Lucinda asked.

"Maybe a little. I can experiment with new recipes, but I'm just not in the mood."

"Oh, you should definitely read those old mystery novels," Stella said, smiling. "The Byrons left them there. Or was it the Reynolds? Sometimes guests leave books behind around the inn too. I still can't believe that bookcase downstairs is a trap door. Anyway, those Agatha Christie novels are fun."

"Is that why Max is reading those mystery books?" I asked.

"He reads?" Jesse joked.

We all laughed and continued to chat about what Jesse should read. It was nice to take a break from the stress of the murder investigation and enjoy each other's company.

As we finished picking the flowers, we went back inside, and Stella showed me how to arrange them into beautiful bouquets. I watched in awe as she effortlessly created the perfect balance of colors and textures.

"You know, Stella," I said, "I think your bouquets could easily be sold as a separate business. They're absolutely stunning. Have you thought about doing dried flower bouquets? They last longer, and I'm sure you can sell them in the gift shop or other shops in town."

Stella blushed at the compliment. "Thank you, Sophie. I've never thought of that. That could be another backup business plan. In case things drag on here at the inn. So much for retirement." She chuckled.

Every so often, I'd look at the door to the downstairs restaurant, hoping Detective Connor would come up again and talk to me. When Stella went to take a nap, I puttered around the garden again, breathing in the fresh air. I sat on the bench lost in my thoughts, and lost track of time. I didn't expect Detective Connor to come by when the sun started to set.

He approached me with a serious look on his face. "Sophie, I'm sorry to interrupt, but I have some news I need to share with you."

I faced him. "What did you find?"

"Exactly as you said. It was definitely an old wine forgery business. We've taken the notebooks we found as evidence."

"Did Lucinda tell you anything?"

"She claims she didn't know about it."

"And you believe her?" I asked.

"That's what I want you to help with. If you hear anything from anyone on the staff, tell me."

He gave me his business card. It included his cell phone number.

"The notebook is dated from over twenty years ago, and I don't know if this person even works here. But just in case you learn something new, call me. And be careful, Sophie. We still don't know who the killer is and if they're still around this inn."

I nodded, feeling a sense of duty. "I'll do whatever I can to help."

"Good," he said, his expression softening. "Thank you."

"I won't let you down, Detective."

He gave me a small smile before standing up to leave. "My team will still be here for a couple more hours, but I have to go back to the station now. Be in touch. And again, be careful. Stay vigilant."

I watched him walk back into the inn. What else could I do to help? Maybe nothing. Or maybe this inn was still full of surprises.

Chapter 10

I didn't know who to begin questioning. Since I was the only one who lived at the inn, albeit temporarily, I was allowed to be on the premises, but most of the staff weren't here. I couldn't think of anyone who would have been involved with this mess. Then again, I didn't know them well since I was so new.

At the front desk, I took a pen and a notepad embossed with the Wildflower Inn logo. I made a list of the staff: Fred, the experienced forty-something chef who Jesse hired for the restaurant in the basement. There was Fred's kitchen crew. James and Eliza were the only full-time waitstaff working there, plus some part-time waitstaff whose name escaped me. Simona, the housekeeper manager, and her team of cleaners. Of course, Lucinda and her crew who worked in the vineyard or nearby wine-making facility on the property. Then there was Marty, the retiree who did odd jobs here for fun. In fact, I had just seen him trimming the bushes in the gardens. Stella or one of her sons must have told him he could hang around as long as he stayed outside and out of the police's way.

As I scanned this list of over two dozen people, I felt a mixture of awe and anxiety. It took so much work and so many people to keep this place running seamlessly. And so many employees' livelihoods depended on the inn. It would break my heart if this murder was the reason for shutting us down.

Out of everyone, I talked to Simona the most. She was closest to me in age, and we got along really well so far. I knew Simona had an older sister who ran a restaurant in town, and Simona often picked up work there when things were slow at the inn or when she needed extra cash. I decided to head over there to talk to her.

I grabbed my purse, threw it over my shoulder, then topped off my outfit of a blue floral sundress with a sunhat. It was only an eight-minute walk to the restaurant and the main strip of the town. The sun was barely peeking through the clouds, and a cool breeze brushed against my face.

I had barely walked beyond the entrance of the inn when a car slowed down next to me. It was Jesse in his beat-up Jeep.

"Going somewhere?" he asked with a small smirk.

"Just walking to town, maybe lunch at Simona's sister's restaurant," I said casually.

"Not dining alone, are you?"

"Not if Simona's around…"

I didn't know whether I should tell him I was really going there so I could ask Simona some questions. I decided not to; it was still better to keep my investigation discreet for now.

"Mind if I come with you?" Jesse asked.

I shrugged. "Sure, why not?"

"I was going to drop off some of Mom's jams to the tea shop, but it'll only take a sec."

That was another thing Stella did, make jams for fun. It seemed like Stella had enough profitable hobbies to start an empire.

"Okay." As I got in the car, I asked, "What was the name of the restaurant again?"

"It's called La Bella Vita. I've only been there once, but great Italian food."

After Jesse ran his errand, we parked in front of La Bella Vita. It was almost lunchtime, and the place was already filling up. When we entered, we were greeted by a tall, slender woman with dark hair pulled back into a bun.

"Are you Simona's sister?" I asked.

"Yes." She gave me a flat smile. "I'm Mariana. And you are?"

"I'm Sophie." I motioned to Jesse behind me. "This is Jesse."

Mariana's expression lit up. She gave Jesse a much friendlier smile. "Yes! Jesse! You had the Al Fredo pasta last week, didn't you?"

Jesse chuckled. "Yeah, that was me. It was amazing."

"We work at the Wildflower Inn with Simona," I said.

"Oh. You work there too? With Jesse?" Mariana fixed me with a questioning look, her eyes narrowing ever-so-slightly.

"Yes, and Simona. I recently started as the reservation manager. She told me about your restaurant. I've heard it's the best Italian in town."

"Thank you." Mariana sounded bored. "Oh, I heard about the death of one of your guests. Was it murder?"

Jesse and I looked at each other. This was a conversation we were not ready to have.

"We don't know," Jesse said slowly. "That's up to the police. Is that what people are talking about?"

"I just heard it from Simona," Mariana said, shooting Jesse another flirtatious smile.

"Do you mind not telling anyone about it?" Jesse said, smiling back. "We don't want gossip to spread when we don't really know what happened."

"Oh, of course not!" Mariana exclaimed. "I haven't told another soul. You can trust me!"

"Good. I'd appreciate that." Jesse grinned. Was he flirting with her?

"Is Simona here?" I asked.

"Not yet. She should be here in half an hour to help with the lunchtime rush. One of our waiters called in sick." Mariana rolled her eyes.

"Well, I'm starved," Jesse said.

Mariana took two menus from the stand. "How's the table by the window?"

"Perfect." Jesse said.

As he pulled out the chair for me, I had to

agree. It was the best spot, with an incredible view of the small town. I'd imagine it would be romantic at night, when the street lanterns were on.

I saw Mariana gazing down at Jesse, admiration glittering in her eyes. As he studied the menu, I took note of his good looks. There was no denying he was attractive with his chiseled jawline, full lips, and bright blue eyes that crinkled when he smiled. But I knew better than to get involved. He was also my boss and coworker, not to mention that I already had a small crush on his brother. After what happened with Ansel, the last thing I needed was more drama in the love department.

Finally, Mariana managed to tear herself away from Jesse. We were left alone to discuss what looked good on the menu. She came back a little too fast with glasses of water for us. Did she pull her black scoop neck shirt lower to show more cleavage? Jesse didn't seem to notice even when she bent down extra low to set down his water. He ordered the lasagna, and I asked for spaghetti bolognese. She was pleasant and laughing whenever he spoke, yet all her charm disappeared with me, her expression becoming a bland mask of indifference.

I was amused, but I also found myself feeling

annoyed. A pang of jealousy seeped in as well. Her flirtations with Jesse made me uneasy. How could she be so forward? Maybe a part of me wished I had the same confidence. And how did she know Jesse wasn't with me? Wasn't that a little presumptuous of her?

We sat in silence as we waited for our food to arrive. Jesse looked at me with his easy smile while I fiddled my fingers on my lap. I was feeling awkward.

"This is so nice," he said as he stared into my eyes. "It's almost like we're on a date."

I felt a blush creep across my face and chest. I hoped it wasn't too noticeable.

"Almost," I said with a chuckle, trying to be as nonchalant as he was. "It is a good date spot."

Mariana kept darting glances over at us even as the restaurant grew busier. She didn't seem to think we were on a date, and I bet she was just waiting for another chance to flirt with Jesse.

He looked at me again and seemed to want to say more, but I dropped my eyes down to the table, suddenly finding the restaurant logo embroidered on the cloth napkin overly fascinating.

When the food arrived, my awkwardness was

overtaken by my hunger. We dug in. I had to admit the bolognese was incredibly delicious.

Halfway through my meal, I looked around the restaurant. "Simona is still not here," I said.

"Did you come just to see her?" Jesse asked.

His eyes were inquisitive, and I knew he was curious about more than just Simona and my friendship. I debated telling him my real intentions —that I was investigating Caleb's death. I looked at him for a moment then decided it was safe to tell him. After all, Detective Connor didn't seem to consider the Amandes suspects, and neither did I. Not really.

"Actually," I began, "I wanted to ask Simona some questions about Caleb, whether she saw or heard anything. I don't think Simona was involved with what happened," I added quickly. "I'm just trying to see if I can get more information to help the police."

"So you *are* going Nancy Drew on me," Jesse sat back, chuckling.

"I know I should be more patient," I said. "But I can't just sit around and do nothing when the inn's closed."

Of course, I didn't mention the part about

Detective Connor asking for my help. Then I would have to explain a lot more to Jesse.

Outside the window, a car pulling into the lot caught my eye. Simona got out of the passenger side. The driver followed. It was Jack, the bartender. When they walked up to the restaurant, they were holding hands.

Chapter 11

J esse turned to look in the direction I was staring.

"I didn't know they were dating," I muttered.

"Oh. I didn't either. Well, it's not against the rules to have employees date as long as they don't bring it into the workplace." He glanced at me as he said it.

Jack and Simona stepped into the restaurant, past a small group waiting for a table. Simona spotted her sister seating to a table near the back and waved. Mariana rushed over to them.

"Thank goodness you're finally here," Mariana said to Simona and Jack. "I'm getting swamped playing double duty as hostess and waitress today."

"I'll get ready right away," Simona said.

"Oh and your friends are here," Mariana said, gesturing to us.

Simona and Jack both turned to face us, their faces lighting up with surprise and delight.

"Hey guys!" Simona exclaimed, a smile spreading across her face. "What are you doing here?"

"We wanted to see you," I said. "Hey Jack."

Jack was tall and muscular, with dirty blonde hair and dark eyes. He had a confidence and ease around other people that came from years of experience as a bartender. He was dressed in a black t-shirt and jeans that hugged his frame, and he looked like he belonged in a magazine. It was easy to see why Simona was attracted to him.

"The food here's amazing," Jesse said. "It looks like we have some competition."

"Nothing beats your pesto pasta," Simona said.

"It is a secret recipe," Jesse said.

"All your recipes seem to be secret," Jack said. "So I guess the cat's out of the bag, huh?"

"What do you mean?" I said innocently.

"Simona and I, we're uh…"

"That's great," Jesse said. "How long has it been?"

"It's new," Simona said. "We didn't want to jinx it. It doesn't go against the employee policies, right? I checked and—"

"It's cool," Jesse said.

"We'd appreciate it if you didn't tell anyone else," Jack said.

"Mum's the word," I said. "I know you guys are busy, but I'd like to talk to you when you get a chance."

"About what happened at the Wildflower Inn?" Simona asked in a hushed tone.

Jesse nodded.

"Sure. I think I can join once you're done with your meal. Just enjoy."

Simona and Jack left us to finish lunch. I had already gotten my fill of food, but dessert was coming. Between trying to investigate this murder and this non-date with Jesse, I was feeling all tangled up inside. The way he looked at me made me feel like there was something printed on my forehead. I felt so embarrassed; his eyes were piercing into me like he could see every thought in my head. I knew I was just being self-conscious, but maybe I wasn't imagining things?

Jesse leaned in closer. "You know, Sophie, I've been meaning to tell you something."

I looked up, meeting his warm gaze. "What is it?" I asked, my voice barely audible.

"I've decided that I'm going to challenge you to a pasta cook-off." Jesse sat back with a grin. "We need to keep busy to pass the time at the inn."

I let out a sigh of relief. "Oh, I don't even know if I can boil a pot of water. I think you'll win by default."

"Cards then? Go Fish tonight?"

"That seems less dangerous." I smiled back. "Deal."

I almost thought he was about to confess his undying love for me or something like that. I was so silly. But there was a part of me that couldn't help but wonder. What if Jesse did have feelings for me? What if I had feelings for him too? It was a strange thought, especially with everything else going on. But for now, I pushed it to the back of my mind and focused on finishing my meal.

Since the lunchtime rush took so long, Jesse and I ended up having a two-hour meal. We had dessert, the tiramisu, a creamy, coffee-flavored dessert served with a dusting of cocoa powder on top. As I took my first bite, I closed my eyes and savored the rich, smooth flavors. Then we had coffee. The beans were from Italy, the best coffee

I've ever drunk. It was the perfect end to a delicious lunch. I was bursting at the seams.

"I'm glad we came here," Jesse said.

"Me too," I replied.

"We should do it more often."

"Hey guys, how was your lunch?" Mariana came by to ask.

"It was great," Jesse replied, before asking for the check. I started reaching for my wallet, but he waved me away, seeming almost offended that I was offering to pay my portion.

"Thanks," I said.

We'd almost forgotten why we came: to question Simona.

After our table was cleared, the restaurant was also starting to clear of the lunchtime crowd. We headed over to the bar where Jack was making drinks for the remaining patrons. Simona was leaning against the counter, taking a breather.

"Hey," Simona said. "How's it going at the inn anyway? Is it going to open up anytime soon?"

"We're hoping it can, but it's up to the police," Jesse said. "And what they can find."

Simona's face fell. "Oh, right," she said, her tone serious. "That whole thing was just so weird. I still can't believe it happened."

"I know, it's crazy," Jesse said, nodding in agreement.

"Do you remember seeing anything strange before or during the day Caleb was found?" I asked.

"Just what I told the police. I didn't really see or hear anything," she said. "I was just cleaning the rooms and making sure my team did."

"Have you ever spoken to Caleb?" I asked.

"No, not really. I've been inside his room. I didn't see anything out of the ordinary either."

"Did you see him speak to anyone else?" I asked.

"No."

"What about anything out of the ordinary in general?" I pressed. "Anything at all."

Simona thought about it. "Well, towards the end of the night, I did notice something weird."

"What was it?" I asked, feeling my heart rate increase.

"I saw a man wearing a hat outside when I was cleaning one of the rooms," Simona said. "It was overlooking the front of the building, not the back gardens. I just thought he had a very old-fashioned hat, in this unusual blue color. Kind of a dark azure. He was talking to someone. I couldn't really see who. The other man was partially obscured, but it could've been Caleb. But then again, it could've been anyone."

"Do you remember what time this was?" I asked.

Simona shook her head. "Sorry, I don't. It was after lunchtime, though. I thought the two men were having a little tiff. The man in the hat seemed to be speaking in a stern voice. I didn't hear what either of them were saying. I was just focused on the hat because it seemed a little old-fashioned."

"Interesting. Did you see anything else?" I asked. "What the guy looked like? What he was wearing?"

"I can't recall. Maybe a dress shirt and pants, but I can't remember the colors. Neutrals. He seemed sort of formal. That's about it. I didn't see or hear anything else unusual."

"Thanks," I said.

When Jack was free, we asked him the same questions. He also didn't interact with Caleb, but he did see the man in the hat that Simona described.

"Yeah, I did see a man like that. He was wearing a suit and a hat, like the ones they wore in the '40s. I couldn't see his face because he had his back towards me, but I remembered he was smoking a cigar. I thought it was strange because I rarely see people smoke cigars. I guess he was pretty old-fashioned."

"Did you see anyone else around?" I asked.

"I think he was talking to someone, but I was just walking past them on my way to work, so I didn't pay attention. There are eccentric guests here all the time."

This man in the hat and suit—I would've remembered a guest like that. Even a patron to the restaurant or a guest at one of the wine tasting events we held. Why hadn't this man enter the inn?

Mariana had her arms crossed, shooting annoyed glances at me as she watched us chat up Jack and Simona. We had to wrap it up. I thanked them both for their help and promised to keep them updated when the inn opened again.

I felt a sense of unease settle over me. Who was the man in the suit and hat? And who had he been talking to? Jesse opened the door for me, and I stepped out of the restaurant. These were questions that needed answers, and I was determined to find them.

Chapter 12

Alone in my bedroom, I sank back into the pillows against the headboard, mulling over the recent events. Jesse and I managed to uncover some new information from Simona and Jack. The description of the hat man they gave was peculiar, yet his connection to Caleb's murder seemed tenuous at best. It might have been nothing at all.

Just as I was about to groan in frustration, a knock on my door interrupted my thoughts.

I opened it to find Max standing there, his eyes tired, hair disheveled. Despite the smile on his face, it seemed a bit strained, as if maintaining it required more effort than usual.

"I hope I'm not interrupting," he said.

"Not at all."

"I was hoping to talk to you about something in private."

"Would you like to come in?" I asked.

He stepped into my bedroom, and I closed the door behind him. We both stood in silence for a moment, taking in the sight of each other.

After what felt like an eternity of silence, I spoke up.

"Is something the matter?"

"Well, I did receive some news. Good news, but unsettling."

"Oh?" I stepped towards him in anticipation.

"The police arrested a suspect in another crime, and they think he could've been Caleb's murderer."

I gasped. "What? Who is it?"

"A local in town named Paul Davis. He was arrested for beating and choking his wife. She's not dead, thankfully, but close to it."

"My goodness," I exclaimed.

"She's in the hospital, barely conscious. If the neighbors hadn't heard her scream and called the police, who knows what he would've done."

My heart sank. Poor woman. Domestic violence wasn't something I had considered in connection with Caleb's murder.

"Was this Paul Davis at the inn recently?"

"He buys wine here all the time, and we have a receipt of him buying wine on the morning of Caleb's murder."

"Okay," I said, mulling this over.

Max shifted from one foot to another. "The police are saying that this could be the break-through they need in the Caleb case…." His voice trailed off as he noticed my expression darken.

Peering out the window, my mind buzzed with questions. Was it possible this Paul Davis was really responsible for Caleb's death? And if so, what could have been his motive? The police seemed to tie him to Caleb's death through the similarity that both involved choking.

But I couldn't shake this feeling in my gut that something wasn't right. There had to be more to the story.

"How old are Paul and his wife?"

"Both around late twenties," Max said.

"Maybe Paul would have a motive in killing Caleb if he was, say, having an affair with his wife, but Caleb's too old."

Max shook his head. "I don't know."

This definitely didn't feel right in my gut.

"The police say we can open the inn again," Max said with a weary but genuine smile.

"That's great," I said flatly.

"Are you okay?"

"I'm just trying to... process everything."

Max nodded but didn't seem convinced. "Well, if you ever need to talk, you know I'm here. The workday is ending, I'll let everyone rest today, but tomorrow, we can start calling the guests at the other inns to let them know it's safe to come back."

Is it really safe, though? I wondered.

"Good. Great. It is great news." I tried to convince Max, and myself.

I had to talk to Detective Connor.

Max turned to leave but lingered at the door. "It's up to the police to make the connection."

Did he sound skeptical too?

"Right. They're the professionals," I said.

"Hey, I heard you went to lunch with Jesse," Max said.

I felt a twinge of discomfort as I nodded. "Yeah. We went to La Bella Vita."

Max looked a little tense. "Jesse seemed to really have enjoyed it."

I was reminded that we had talked to Simona and Jack, and what they had told us.

"By the way, what does Paul Davis look like?" I asked Max.

"Like I said, he's in his late twenties. Usually walks around town with a scruffy beard and one of his metal band T-shirts. On the shorter side. Pudgy. You've seen him?"

I shook my head. "So he's definitely not someone who would be wearing a suit?"

"Like a tailored suit?"

"Maybe from the '40s or '50s? With a fedora?"

Max furrowed his brow. "That sounds pretty specific. Why do you ask?"

I took a deep breath and explained what Simona and Jack had said at lunch, about the man in the suit and hat who had been hanging around outside the inn.

"That's definitely not Paul Davis," Max said. "He's nothing like that."

"Right," I said. "But who is this man in the suit? And why was he here that day? The same day Caleb was murdered."

Max absentmindedly glanced at the photos on the wall. He stepped inside again and pointed to the main photograph of the Reynolds family.

"Are you talking about this kind of suit?" He was pointing to the patriarch of the family.

I stood up to examine the photos on the gallery wall closely. The man in the photo, Mr. Reynolds, was indeed wearing a suit with a fedora. "Yes, I think so."

"Well, Mr. Reynolds must have passed by now. His children are in retirement age." He hesitated for a moment before continuing. "I've heard rumors that the Reynolds family was involved in some shady business dealings. Some people even say they were connected to organized crime."

"Why didn't you say anything before?"

"I didn't know until after we bought the business. It was just rumors I heard around town though. Nothing was ever proven. I didn't want our inn to be associated with any of those rumors, so I didn't spread that gossip to the staff."

"That's understandable. But are you saying that this mystery man might be connected to the Reynolds family?" I asked. "Or even part of the Reynolds family?"

"We don't want to jump to any conclusions without more evidence,"he said. "After all, the police did arrest a suspect."

"Maybe it's the ghost of Mr. Reynolds," I joked.

Max laughed, but we both looked at his picture again in contemplative silence.

"It may be flimsy," Max said, "but it's something we can look into."

We looked at each other. I nodded. "Let's start by looking into the Reynolds family history. Maybe we can find some connections to this mystery man."

Chapter 13

Although I wanted to play cards with Jesse, both of us had pressing matters to attend to. Max and I decided to kick off our investigation by searching the internet. Meanwhile, Stella needed Jesse's help to bottle and label a fresh batch of her famous blueberry jams for sale. They needed to make up for the lost income at the inn.

In Max's cozy office, it was just the two of us, heads bent over our laptops, digging for clues and leads. Side by side, we scoured ancestry databases, local history forums, and genealogy blogs, searching for anyone who might have connections to the Reynolds family. Unfortunately, none of those places led me to anything, given the multitude of people named Reynolds.

Turning to Facebook, I looked for anyone who might have worked for the Wildflower Inn. Eventually, I got a lead from a woman named Beth Greene, who had once briefly worked as a receptionist when the Reynolds offspring, Stephen and Beatrice, were in charge. In her profile picture, Beth appeared to be a beaming grandmother of five.

I messaged her. She was online and responded promptly. Beth was more than happy to connect us with a former employee who had worked there longer. When she asked about our research, I explained that it was for the history of the inn for marketing purposes—a good enough reason for her to direct us to a former colleague, likely just a Facebook friend to Beth nowadays.

Clark Higgins, a retired head waiter from our inn, now living two towns over, agreed to meet at a greasy spoon diner close to his house that evening. He gave us directions to a small town called Woodbury.

The drive took an hour, but the lovely scenery during sunset and Max's company made it enjoyable. Woodbury, although smaller than Sierra Hills, had a similarly captivating charm. We passed the downtown area with mom-and-pop shops and cozy cafes, and I made mental notes of places to explore when I got my own car. The heart of the town was marked by a beautiful fountain, surrounded by benches where locals probably gathered and socialized on sunny days.

We parked in front of the diner, the neon sign flickering above us. As soon as we walked through the door, I was hit by the enticing smell of burgers. The hostess led us to a back booth where we found Clark doing the crossword in the newspaper. A warm smile spread across his face as he stood up to greet us with a firm handshake.

"I'm glad you could meet with us, Mr. Higgins," Max said.

"Please, call me Clark," he replied with a kind smile. "Aren't you a fine young couple."

Max and I exchanged a look, and we laughed awkwardly, choosing not to correct him. His assumption could work in our favor.

We exchanged pleasantries, surrounded by the comforting chatter of other patrons. Clark and Max only had pie, while I indulged in a burger and a chocolate milkshake.

Clark shared stories about his retired life, spending most days perfecting his golf swing and volunteering at the local community center. We listened patiently even though we were eager to learn about his time with the Reynolds family. However, we let him talk, to make him feel comfortable with us.

After finishing my burger, I finally asked him the real reason we were there. "Have you heard any stories or rumors when you worked at the Wildflower Inn?"

"So, you want to know about the Reynolds family, eh? What is this for, exactly?"

I had a whole story prepared about research for a marketing campaign promoting the inn's legacy history, but looking into his eyes, I decided to be honest.

We explained the mysterious death of one of our guests and our efforts to uncover information about the Reynolds family, known for shady business dealings. The two might be connected.

As Clark's eyes widened, he leaned in closer to us, his curiosity and hesitation evident. After a brief moment, Clark finally spoke up.

"I heard things," he said. "But I wasn't one for gossip. Maybe I didn't want to know. Beatrice and Stephen did have some financial trouble at some point, but the staff always got paid."

He paused, thinking, and then added, "But I might have some information that could help."

Max and I exchanged a look, wondering what it could be. Max insisted on paying for the meal, and Clark gave us directions to his house on the outskirts of town, although we had no trouble following his car in ours.

He opened the door to his garage. It was so full of stuff, I bet he never even parked his car in there. It just wouldn't fit.

We followed him past stacked boxes and things like dusty old ski equipment until Clark stopped to proudly show us an old wooden chest. He said that it once belonged to the Reynolds family. He had acquired it during an estate sale held by the Byrons before the renovations.

"Why did you buy it?" I asked.

"I guess I'm sentimental. I worked there for twelve years."

Clark opened the chest, allowing us to look through old documents, invoices, and receipts. Among the stacks of papers, he found a letter.

"I always thought this letter was interesting. I'm surprised the Reynolds even kept it. Maybe it was misplaced and they forgot to get rid of it."

He gave me the letter to read. It was addressed

to the Reynolds family from a man named John Glenn, demanding money for something gone wrong. It was vaguely worded and politely threatening.

"This could be something," I said, passing the letter to Max.

Max's face turned serious as he read the letter. "Do you know anything about this John Glenn?" he asked Clark.

"I remember overhearing something about John when I worked at the inn. He did something with wine distribution, but I never actually saw him bring wine. He often came to visit the Reynolds family. He seemed a bit shady, and I never knew what he wanted from them, but I keep my nose out of things, so I never asked."

"What did he look like?"

"Tall, thin nose. Average looking, although distinguished. He must've been in his fifties at the time."

"Did he like to wear hats?" I asked. "Fedora type hats?"

"Hats?" Clark thought about it. "Not often, but maybe he did when it rained. I can't remember."

Clark didn't seem to know much more than that. He let us keep the letter and decided we could take all the documents from the chest. If we didn't find anything helpful, we could discard them, but Clark insisted we keep them for archival purposes.

"My wife will be pleased," he said. "I've been promising to clear out this garage for seven years. She can finally use this chest for her knitting supplies."

"Thanks," Max said.

"Yes. Good luck, Clark," I said.

We promised to keep him updated on any new information. As we drove back to the inn, I felt we were getting closer to solving the mystery. However, the more we uncovered, the more questions arose.

Chapter 14

The next morning, the inn was bustling with guests once again. The staff was back, and everyone was happy and relieved. After breakfast, Max, Jesse, and I carved out some free time to look into the mysterious letter. We estimated that John Glenn, if still alive, would be in his seventies or eighties, but we had no idea if he was still living in Sierra Hills.

"Maybe someone in town or a neighboring town might have some information on him," Max suggested.

"Yes, and he might still have relatives around here," I added.

"Let's make this a competition," Jesse said. "Whoever finds dirt on John Glenn gets a...," he paused, searching for a fitting prize, "…gets a free night's stay at the inn!" He chuckled, since we all lived on the property.

I still needed to find my own apartment. Stella lived in a lovely house adjacent to the inn. Max and Jesse were temporarily living there. They both needed to find their own places too. Once Jesse had complained that while living with their mother had its perks, he felt like he had regressed back to childhood.

Max and Jesse were stuck sharing the same computer, which led to brotherly bickering between them. Jesse, being the more impatient one, would complain that Max wasn't typing fast enough. Max would annoy him further by typing even slower.

I tried to focus on my research, but their brother banter became quite the distraction. I didn't know whether to chastise them for not taking their work seriously or laugh at their childlike behavior. But the bond between the two brothers was undeniable; they were like two peas in a pod, always teasing and joking. Maybe it was true that living together, plus working together so closely, made them regress into little boys.

Attempting to concentrate again, I plunged back into my research. Social media once again came to our aid, leading us to a woman on Face-book with the last name Glenn. Nancy Glenn was a woman in her fifties working at the local beauty salon.

"She has to be related to John," I exclaimed to Max and Jesse. "There are no other Glenns in Sierra Hills on Facebook."

"There are some Glenns in neighboring towns," Jesse said. "No John Glenns, so maybe you can question this Nancy first."

"If she doesn't know who John is, we'll try the other Glenns," Max added. "Although I hope she does, since there are a lot of Glenns around."

"Okay," I said. "I'm calling for an appointment."

"What appointment?" Jesse asked.

"A hair appointment." I thought it was obvious. "She works at The Lilac Salon in town."

"I've seen that place," Max said.

"I need a haircut anyway," I said, idly playing with my long brown hair. Did I have split ends? I couldn't even remember the last time I had it cut.

"You sure you don't want one of us to come with you?" Max asked.

"I'm sure. Women open up to each other at these places."

I hoped I was right.

———

ENTERING through the glass doors of The Lilac Salon, I was immediately embraced by a warm and inviting atmosphere. Laughter and chatter filled the air, accompanied by the sweet fragrance of hair products. The lilac-colored walls created a serene ambiance amidst the bustling scene.

The receptionist led me to Nancy's station. As I walked past the lively clients in the salon, I couldn't help but smile at the familiar sounds of gossip. One woman exclaimed, "I can't believe she actually said that!" while others shook their heads, saying things like, "The nerve of some people."

Nancy, a kind-looking woman with curly brown hair touched with gray, introduced herself. She looked every bit the chic older woman I aspired to be one day in her crisp white blouse and black trousers. When she leaned in, her hair carried the scent of lilac, the salon's signature fragrance.

Nancy turned me around to the mirror. As I looked into my big brown eyes and stringy hair, she asked, "So, what kind of haircut are we looking for today?"

After a brief moment of thought, I replied, "I want something fresh and new, maybe shoulder-length with some layers."

Nancy nodded in approval. "I think I know just what to do. How about some highlights as well? They would really bring out your natural hair color."

"That sounds perfect," I replied, feeling excited about the new look. A young woman led me to the shampoo station, where I indulged in the luxury of having my hair lathered and massaged. I almost forgot why I was there.

Back in Nancy's chair, she went to work with her shears. We chatted about the salon, the town, and her family. Nancy, a Sierra Hills native, had never ventured far from home. Through her job, she practically knew every resident of Sierra Hills or at least something about them.

I mentioned my recent move to town for my job at the Wildflower Inn.

"Of course, I know the Wildflower Inn. It has changed owners a few times, hasn't it?"

"Yeah, the new owners seem to be doing well. Very entrepreneurial," I replied.

Nancy hummed as she worked on my hair.

"That's good to hear. The previous owners didn't seem to like all the work of the inn."

"I heard that too. It does take quite a few people to keep that place running smoothly." I shared a bit more about the Amandes and mentioned Stella. "You'll probably meet her soon. I'll recommend The Lilac Salon to her."

"Thank you."

"Have you been to the inn recently?" I asked. "I'm sure you would know quite a few people who work there. It's a big staff."

"Well, you're right about that. Everyone around here seems to know everyone else's business," she said, chuckling.

And she was right. She told me that Simona and Eliza came here all the time. I asked her if she knew any former employees as well, friends or family.

Nancy paused, her scissors still in hand. "Why do you ask?" she inquired, her tone suddenly guarded.

I shrugged nonchalantly, even though my heart rate quickened. "Just curious, I guess. I'm new in town and trying to get a sense of the community and who knows who."

Nancy hesitated before finally responding. "I do

know some people who used to work for the previous owners, the ones who built the place. The Reynolds? I didn't hear very good things."

Intrigued, I raised an eyebrow. "What kind of things did you hear?" I prodded.

Chapter 15

Nancy worked her magic with the scissors, shaping my hair into an elegant and modern silhouette. Pausing, she glanced around the salon, making sure our conversation was safe from prying ears.

"Well, let's just say that the Reynolds were involved in some questionable business dealings. Some folks in town suspected them of money laundering and fraud," she whispered, eyes flitting around the room. "Nothing was ever proven, and they sold the inn and hightailed out of town."

"Do you think the new owners are aware of this?" I asked.

Nancy shrugged. "I have no idea. They're from out of town, right? Probably saw a good deal and snapped it up. When the Byrons took over, the inn seemed like an honest business. They were doing well. They just weren't cut out for running a place that big."

"Right. They wanted to retire. Not to mention, keeping the guests happy can take patience, even though most of them are lovely."

"Didn't I hear that there was some police there the other day?" Nancy asked. "What's that about?"

I breathed a sigh of relief; news about the murder hadn't traveled that far. If the ladies at the hair salon were still in the dark, we were in the clear, especially now that the inn was back up and running.

"Yes," I replied. "They asked some questions about Paul Davis, who bought wine in our store."

Of course, I had to leave out the part about Caleb.

"Oh yes! Mrs. Montgomery was telling me about that horrible man this morning. Choking his wife. Can you imagine? I hope he gets his due. I should go check in on his poor wife."

I murmured my agreement.

"But what can be done about it now?" She continued. "I hope she has the support she needs. There's a women's shelter in town. I'm sure she has plenty of people to stay with, but she could get support there if anything."

A heavy weight settled in my chest. Even my own struggles with Ansel, who had never been physically violent, must have paled in comparison to what this woman endured. I couldn't even begin to imagine the pain she must have experienced. Sensing my unease, Nancy quickly changed the subject, breaking the tension.

"Did you catch a glimpse of Detective Connor?" she asked. "He's quite the dish, isn't he?"

I laughed. "He has nice eyes. Kind of serious, but kind."

"You talked to him?"

"I kind of had to."

"You're lucky." Nancy winked at me in the mirror. "He's single, you know."

"Why is that?"

"Oh, he had a sweetheart, but she moved away a couple of years ago. I guess it didn't work out. He's one of those men who works too much. Maybe that was why they broke up."

I nodded, thinking about Detective Connor and how grim and serious he always looked. But the last time we spoke, he seemed encouraging and even gentle. I wondered if…

"If you're interested, you should make your move," Nancy said. "Half these ladies are in line, hoping to date him." She gestured to the women at the salon, chuckling.

"I'll think about it." I laughed back.

I was getting distracted again. I directed the conversation back to who she knew who worked at the inn.

"You said you knew some friends who used to work at the inn?" I asked. "Or relatives?"

"Oh, it was a long time ago. I have this uncle, John, who used to work with them. But John was kind of a black sheep of the family. He traveled a lot. Still does. He's quite the character."

"Wow. And he worked at the inn?"

"Well, He did his own thing. He was an importer-exporter of whatever was hot. Toys, gadgets, even cheese once. He sold wine to the inn or something. Something to do with wine anyway. He loved wine in general, always bringing back different kinds from different countries."

"Where did he travel to?"

"He was often in Europe—Monaco and the French Riviera, mainly. And he traveled around Italy, Spain, even Austria and Germany." Nancy laughed. "I haven't seen him for years."

"Really. He doesn't come to town often?"

"No. I don't know where he is now, but he's probably living it up somewhere. I wouldn't be surprised if he is still traveling around, looking for the next hot thing to sell. Oh, my customers usually do most of the talking, but here I am babbling on. What about you, dear? Why did you take this job in Sierra Hills of all places?"

I wasn't used to sharing my personal life with strangers, but something about Nancy made me feel comfortable. Maybe it was the fact that she was so easy to talk to or that she reminded me of my aunt. Whatever it was, I found myself opening up to her, even though I only mentioned wanting a fresh start after a breakup.

"Good for you, dear. Everyone deserves that. You'll love Sierra Hills."

"I love it already," I said.

"There's a lot to do. Have you been to Patty's Pilates?"

As she talked, I thought about her uncle John. Could he be the one who was brokering deals for the fake wine? Did he even make the fake wine? If so, why didn't the Reynolds family pay him properly?

It all seemed to add up! I couldn't wait to share

my theory with Max and Jesse, and even fill in Detective Connor on my findings.

Nancy blow-dried my hair. It looked great that I almost gasped when I looked up at the mirror. The layers gave my hair volume and movement, and the highlights added a subtle shimmer.

"I love it!" I exclaimed, twirling around in the chair to get a better look. My hair just grazed my shoulders now, and I felt so light. "Nancy. You're a true artist."

Nancy beamed with pride. "You look gorgeous! It was a pleasure having you today. Don't be a stranger, okay?"

I promised her I wouldn't and made my way to the receptionist to pay.

I RETURNED to the Wildflower Inn with a newfound sense of confidence. The fresh cut made me feel like a whole new person. As I strolled by the front garden, I caught sight of Jesse carrying a basket of carrots, about to head inside. His eyes widened in surprise as he took in my new look. A grin spread across his face, and he gave a whistle of approval.

"Wow. You look incredible."

I felt my cheeks flush with pleasure. "Thanks. Nancy did an amazing job."

"Yeah, I can tell. It suits you so well."

We walked in together. Max was at the front desk to fill in for me.

"Sophie? You look so…different."

"Better, I hope."

"Really…pretty." He looked shy as he said it.

I beamed.

Jesse leaned in, taking an exaggerated whiff of my hair. "You smell like lilacs."

"Don't be weird," Max teased, playfully shoving Jesse's arm away.

I ran my fingers through my freshly cut hair. It felt so silky. I should really go back and buy their hair products too.

"Actually, while I was there, I found out something pretty important." My voice dropped to a hushed tone as I led Jesse and Max back into Max's office.

I told them all about what I learned about Nancy's uncle John.

Chapter 16

I found myself in Max's spacious office, absentmindedly tracing the shapes of the countries on a world map adorning one wall. Jesse leaned casually against a bookshelf, pushing his sandy blond hair out of his eyes. Max sat at his desk, the laptop screen illuminating his handsome features.

"John Glenn," I murmured, my eyes scanning the map. "He could be in Europe, but then again, he could be anywhere."

"He's not an easy man to find," Max admitted, leaning back with frustration.

"We'd need to join the CIA to track him down," I quipped.

"Or he's just exceptionally good at hiding,"

Jesse added, a mischievous twinkle in his eyes. "Maybe he's really the international spy, or a James Bond villain."

"Jesse, we don't have time for jokes," Max scolded, though I couldn't help but crack a smile— Jesse's irreverence was infectious.

"I'm just trying to lighten the mood," Jesse said, grinning. "We'll find him, Sophie. We just need to keep digging or ask around town."

"He could've easily changed his name," Max mused.

"Even if he didn't, John Glenn is a common name," I sighed.

Footsteps outside grabbed our attention. Max glanced at me before suggesting, "Hey guys, it's almost lunchtime. Maybe one of us should head out to the front desk in case any of our new guests need help."

"I should check on the kitchen staff," Jesse chimed in. "Make sure nothing's on fire."

I rose, straightening my pencil skirt. Work should be my priority, and the inn's 70% occupancy rate post-murder meant we needed to keep guests happy.

"No, you can stay," Max said to me. "I'll be out.

You keep investigating. You're better at this than I am."

"Really?"

"Sure. I think we're close to figuring this out. Keep at it."

"I guess I can check more social media sites."

Max patted me on the shoulder as he left.

"Good luck." Jesse winked.

Alone, I settled into my seat, determination filling me. Max's words bolstered my confidence.

I thought about what Nancy had said about her elusive uncle. I realized he wouldn't easily disclose his whereabouts, even to family. She hardly traveled, so she wouldn't have visited him. They didn't sound close at all. Nancy made it seem as though he appeared in town randomly whenever it suited him.

"The last time could've been Caleb's murder," I muttered. "He'd probably long skipped town by now."

I considered returning to The Lilac Salon to ask Nancy more questions under the excuse of getting a blowout. John Glenn held the key, but revealing my suspicions about her uncle felt awkward. Was I supposed to tell her I seriously suspected that her uncle was a thief and killer? Would that make her help me? Maybe she would help the police. And the police, particularly Detective Connor with his authoritative presence, could make her talk.

As I reached for the office phone, hesitation set in. No, I wanted to talk to Detective Connor in person. Not because he had mesmerizing green eyes —my intentions were purely professional. Besides, we had more privacy at the police station.

With newfound energy, I practically skipped to my room to get my purse... and put on some lip gloss.

However, just as I was about to enter, something on the floor caught my eye. A neatly folded piece of paper lay before me. I crouched down to pick it up, unfolding it carefully, wondering who it was from.

The note was written in a deliberate, blocky script, sending a shiver down my spine:

"STOP THE INVESTIGATION IF YOU VALUE YOUR LIFE."

It was written on the inn's stationery.

Chapter 17

I clutched the rough paper, each word carving itself into my mind. My breaths quickened as I frantically looked around the room. Sweat dripped down my forehead as I struggled to control my fear. Who in this inn could possibly know about my investigation?

Was this person a new arrival, or had they been here all along, surreptitiously watching me? Could it possibly be John Glenn himself, hiding in plain sight?

A sense of being watched crept over me, as if a pair of unseen eyes were boring into the back of my neck.

My eyes scanned the room, seeking any clues of intrusion or disruption. Could someone have broken in during the short hour I was away? My gaze landed on the window and I hurried over to inspect it. It remained firmly locked, without any evidence of a break-in.

The killer must have just slipped the note under the door.

Or they could still be lurking in the room, hiding under the bed or inside the closet. Or worse, they could be waiting outside, biding their time for me to make a move.

Maybe investigating on my own had been a terrible idea. I was an amateur. I should prioritize my safety above everything else. Perhaps I really should end my investigation. This was not worth putting my life at risk.

The memory of Caleb's lifeless body flashed in my mind. How the fate of the inn had hung in the balance, employees risking being out of work. The killer was still at large, a danger to everyone here. I couldn't leave, not with so much at stake.

"Be brave, Sophie," I whispered to myself.

I took a deep breath. Whoever left the note wanted me to be afraid, to give up. But I wouldn't give them that satisfaction. If someone was threatening me to stop investigating, it meant that I was getting too close to the truth.

With shaking hands, I opened my closet door, ready to punch someone if they sprang out.

Nothing but my clothes.

I checked under the bed.

Nothing but dust balls.

The killer wasn't here. I was safe in this room. For now.

I found Detective Connor's business card on one of the night stands to call him, pacing my small room feeling like a caged bird. I dialed the personal cell number that was on the card.

"Detective Connor," his deep voice answered, offering an odd sense of comfort.

"Detective, it's Sophie," I stammered. I struggled to find my words as I frantically told him about the note and the possible presence of the killer in the inn. "Can you please send someone over?"

"Stay calm, Sophie," he instructed, concern lacing his tone. "I'm on my way. In the meantime, be close to the brothers and don't go anywhere alone."

"Thank you, Detective," I whispered, my voice quivering. I ended the call and rushed out, wanting to be around Max and Jesse.

As soon as I opened the door, a dark figure materialized in front of me, barring my way. He was about average height, dressed entirely in black with a ski mask concealing his face. My heart raced and my mouth turned dry with terror. The killer had found me.

"Who are you?" I demanded, my voice wavering despite my best efforts to remain strong. "What do you want?"

"Your silence," the figure hissed, their voice distorted low to hide their identity. "You're getting too close to the truth, Sophie."

My mind raced, searching for a way out of this life-threatening situation. I snatched the lamp from the bedside table and flung it at the figure with all my might. The sound of breaking glass echoed through the room.

I lunged forward, my hand snatching a shard of glass from the broken lamp. With trembling fingers, I brandished it like a makeshift dagger, trying to project confidence in my voice as I warned, "Stay back!"

The figure sneered, unfazed by my makeshift weapon. "What then?" they challenged.

"I'll scream louder," I replied, my eyes brimming with tenacity. "This place has ears, you know. Help!"

The commotion caught the attention of the

Amandes brothers. I heard their hurried steps echoing down the hallway towards my room. In a moment of chaos and distraction, I seized the opportunity to slip past the intruder and make my escape to Max and Jesse.

"Jesse, get him!" Max commanded. They both charged after the man in the ski mask.

From my spot in the hallway, I could hear the scuffle and struggle as Max and Jesse fought with the intruder. The sound of fists connecting with flesh reverberated through the walls, punctuated by grunts of exertion and pain. For a split second, I hesitated, uncertain if I should go back and join in the fight. But it was two against one, and the masked man seemed to be unarmed. He didn't stand a chance against them.

But out of nowhere, the intruder broke free from Max's grip and charged towards Jesse. Reacting with lightning speed, Jesse evaded the attack and landed a devastating punch to the intruder's jaw, knocking him off balance. Seizing the opportunity, Max swiftly tackled the intruder to the ground, subduing him.

Jesse stepped forward, landing a powerful kick to the intruder's ribs. The intruder let out a loud grunt of pain before going momentarily still. Max quickly took advantage of this opportunity, pinning the intruder to the ground and delivering a final blow that rendered him unconscious.

Swiftly snapping out of my shock, I frantically dialed 9-1-1. I knew Detective Connor was still on the way, but I had to do something. I hoped Max and Jesse weren't hurt. They had saved my life.

Chapter 18

Detective Connor's polished leather shoes clicked against the wooden floorboards as he strode into the inn. Two policemen followed him inside. I saw his intense green eyes scanning the area, then resting on my trembling figure on the staircase.

"Detective Connor, thank goodness you're here," I said. "The killer… he's inside one of the guest rooms!"

"Which room?" Detective Connor asked.

"My room. Room 23."

The detective ran up the stairs with his colleagues. I followed closely behind. My nerves were rattled, but I wanted to see who the killer was.

Jesse and Max were still in my room, tying the

intruder up with the cord that was used to tie the window curtains.

They had pulled the ski mask off the intruder and I gasped when I saw who he was.

Marty Johnson. His once neat and tidy white hair was now a mess. His eyes slowly blinked, going in and out of consciousness.

"Marty?" I couldn't believe it.

Even Detective Connor seemed taken aback. "Marty Johnson!" he exclaimed.

"Do you know him?" Max asked.

"Just that he's a retired businessman." Detective Connor replied. "Does lots of charity work. Never caused any problems."

We stared at Marty in disbelief. I wondered how Stella would handle this news.

Marty's eyelids fluttered open, his gaze landing on the faces hovering above him. Furrowing his brow in confusion, he tried to sit up but the ropes around his wrists and ankles held him tightly in place.

"What's going on?" he groaned, struggling against his restraints.

Detective Connor leaned forward, his voice unwavering and controlled as he read him his Miranda rights.

Marty's eyes widened in disbelief and shock as he listened. But then a self-realization seemed to set in.

"Why?" I asked. "Why did you do it?"

"It wasn't my intention," Marty explained. "We had a fight, and I may have gotten carried away."

"You think?" Max muttered.

Detective Connor arched an eyebrow. "What was the cause of the altercation?"

Marty looked at the detective, the policemen, the Amandes brothers, and me, holding his note, and sighed.

"I had overheard him talking to Stephen Reynolds outside the inn. I guess he was old friends with Caleb. Stephen and Caleb had a lunch in town or something and Stephen dropped Caleb off back in front of the inn. Before he drove off, he lingered around for a smoke and asked Caleb to do something for him. I was helping Stella prune the front garden, and the bushes hid me well, but I was able to hear most of what they were saying. Stephen wanted to check if there was still this room in the restaurant in the basement. A hidden room. He wanted to see if there were still a bunch of wine in there. I heard him say the names of a bunch of wines, and from what I knew, they were some of the most expensive wines out there.

"He handed Caleb a map and whispered to him how to access it. I didn't hear that part, but I thought it was exciting, how there was a room with all these rare wines. So I followed Caleb around. Finally, when the inn cleared of guests having lunch, I saw him head downstairs. I knew there would be no one else down in the restaurant, so I followed him. I didn't have a plan, exactly, I just wanted to see the wines. But Caleb noticed me, and he demanded to know what I was doing down there. I told him that I heard about the note, and I wanted to see the wines too, but Caleb got angry. He wouldn't let me see the map! I tried to grab it from him. He pushed me. So we got into a fight. I didn't mean mean to choke him to death, I really didn't…"

Marty broke into a sob.

"But the wines are fakes," I said.

"What?" Marty looked up at me.

"It was a room to forge expensive wine."

"So there wasn't anything expensive in there?"

"No," Detective Connor said. "Someone would've taken the expensive wines when the

Reynolds sold this place. I'm surprised they left the room as it was though."

"Maybe he wanted to start up on the business again," Jesse suggested. "Just in case he needed to."

Detective Connor looked Marty in the eye. "Was it worth it?"

Marty was still sobbing. "I was just looking for a bit of adventure. I was so bored in my retirement. A secret room full of expensive wines was something I wanted to take a peek at."

"And steal the wine?" the detective said.

Marty looked down. He didn't answer.

"Why did you threaten me?" I shook the note in the hand.

He looked up at me. "When I found out you three were digging into things, I panicked. I just wanted to scare you."

I shook my head. What an amateur. He was a terrible criminal.

Max looked at me and then narrowed his eyes at him. "I hope you got the adventure you were looking for."

"Stella," Marty moaned to himself, his voice thick with emotion. "Tell your mother I never meant for any of this to happen. It was all an accident!"

Marty had ruined his chances with Stella forever.

————

DETECTIVE CONNOR TOLD us that he had looked into John Glenn already, based on what he could gleam from the papers and notebooks he found in the hidden wine duplication room. Glenn was long gone. Definitely changed his name. Disappeared without a trace.

He was more than likely the person who was making the fakes for the Reynolds. Given his connections, he probably went abroad to sell it. At some point his business partnership with the Reynolds soured. They owed him money, and in turn, he must've taken all the real wine. He didn't really need the Reynolds other than the hidden room they provided, so he struck out on his own. Maybe he was still out there somewhere making fake wine.

The Reynolds siblings, still deeply in debt, reluctantly put the inn up for sale. With their meager profits, they retired to a quiet life, hoping to make ends meet. None of the townspeople had heard from them since they left. Maybe they went into hiding too. Maybe Stephen came to town just to catch up with his old friend Caleb, and curiosity prompted him to visit the inn, but he probably didn't want to step inside or explore the property in case he ran into his old employees who would recognize him.

The Wildflower Inn definitely had a fascinating history. The police had cleared out all the evidence in the hidden cellar, and now we were left with an extra room.

"What do we do with it?" Jesse asked.

After a moment of contemplation, I spoke up. "We should use it for a similar purpose, but without any unethical dealings. We could turn it into a wine cellar for rare and exquisite wines."

Max nodded approvingly. "That's a great idea."

Jesse grinned. "I can see it now. 'The Glenn Cellar'."

"The Glenn Cellar at the Wildflower Inn. It has a nice ring to it." I said, chuckling.

"There's no way we're going to call it that," Max said.

We all laughed.

Chapter 19

The once chaotic atmosphere of the inn had finally settled back into the familiar routine I used to adore. The aroma of freshly brewed coffee wafted through the air, along with the gentle hum of conversations between contented guests enjoying their breakfast. The sturdy wooden tables were surrounded by plush chairs invitingly beckoning visitors to sink in and savor a hot latte or cocoa.

I made my way to the counter and poured myself a cup of coffee, relishing in its welcoming scent as I indulged in each sip. My gaze swept over the room, finding comfort in the sight of familiar faces who had come to call this inn their home away from home.

I smiled. Everything was as it should be. I finally felt at home in this cozy inn.

I spotted a vacant table next to the wide-open window and made my way over, taking in the serene garden views. The melodious chirping of birds and gentle rustling of leaves provided tranquil background noise. But Stella's presence caught my attention. She hauled a tray of scrumptious cinnamon rolls and piled them onto a large plate on the breakfast buffet table.

"Need any help?" I asked.

"No dear. You enjoy your breakfast before your shift starts."

I smiled as I watched Stella, her white hair framing her face like a halo. The mischievous sparkle had returned to her blue eyes after the recent events involving her friend Marty. Something in the way she moved told me that she was going to be okay.

After returning the tray to the kitchen, she took a seat across from me at the table. Without any prompting, she began opening up about Marty and everything that had happened between them. I could see the emotions bubbling just beneath the surface as she spoke.

"Never would have guessed he was the one behind it all." Stella shook her head.

"Did you know him well?" I asked.

"Not really," she replied with a heavy sigh. "He started coming around more often after we bought the inn. We thought he was just a regular and let him help out. He never asked for any money. His wife died four years ago...poor guy must've lost his way without her."

I shook my head too, still trying to wrap my head around the fact that Marty, of all people, had been the criminal we'd been searching for.

Initially, Marty appeared friendly enough, however I should have been more wary when I saw him sneaking into Caleb's room. He had too much access to the inn as an unofficial employee. I had thought it was okay because I assumed he and Stella were dating.

However, I wondered why did he feel the need to enter after committing the heinous act of murder? Wasn't that enough? I asked Stella.

"He was stealing," she said, her voice trembling with dismay. "I caught him red-handed once, taking an expensive belt from the lost and found bin. At first, I wanted to believe it was a mistake, that he just liked the belt and assumed no one was going to claim it. But then I started noticing things. Guests would come and report missing items from their rooms— combs, souvenirs, you name it. And I couldn't shake off the suspicion that Marty was responsible."

"He must've been really bored in retirement," I said. "He sounds like a teenager learning the thrill of shoplifting for the first time."

"I wanted to fire him. Well, he wasn't on the payroll, but I wanted to tell him to stop coming around, but he seemed to have nothing better to do, so I felt sorry for him. I was working up the nerve to confront him about the stealing, but then the murder happened. If I had only found the guts to tell him to leave, this tragedy could've been avoided."

I reached out to squeeze Stella's hand, offering her what little comfort I could. "Don't blame yourself, Stella. The man was dangerous."

"I was the one closest to him. I should have been more aware."

"You've only been running the inn for a few weeks," I said. "You couldn't have known him that well."

There was a moment of silence as she processed my words.

"So you weren't...dating?" I broached the subject as carefully as I could. She was my boss after all, but I really wanted to know.

"Heavens, no." Stella didn't seem to know whether to act horrified to amused.

"Ah, sorry. I thought Marty had a little crush on you."

"I never really saw him as more than a friend," Stella added thoughtfully. "He's really not my type. Plus, my husband passed away less than a year ago. I'm not ready to date anyone."

"Right." I trailed off, feeling awkward discussing the love life of my boss.

Stella met my gaze. "Actually, what about you, Sophie? What's your type?"

I blushed, caught off guard. "I don't really have a type," I said.

"Everyone has a type," Stella teased, leaning in closer to me. "Come on, spill the beans. Take my sons for example. Are you more into the strong silent type like Max, or the funny goofball like Jesse?"

"I mean…" I felt my cheeks growing hot. "I don't really know them that well."

Stella chuckled. "Well, let me tell you a little secret. Max may seem like a tough guy, but he's really a softie at heart. And Jesse might come off as a goofball, but he's also very intelligent. They're both good catches in their own ways."

It was clear that she adored her sons. Was it all in good fun, or did she genuinely want me to pursue a relationship with one of them? Regardless, like Stella, I wasn't ready to dive into romance just yet. For the time being, I was content being a part of their world, working alongside the Amandes towards the success of the Wildflower Inn.

"It's shocking that they're both still single," I remarked. "And with all the gorgeous women in this town and coming through the inn, you'd think they would have been snatched up by now."

"They're each waiting for that special one," Stella said, that twinkle of mischief still in her eyes. "They want someone who can keep up with them intellectually and emotionally."

We were interrupted by Jesse's loud voice echoing from the kitchen counter. "Hey, Sophie!" He frantically waved a wooden spoon in my direction. "Could you do me a favor and taste this tomato sauce? It's for the pasta we're having for lunch and I need to make sure it's just right."

"Sure." I excused myself.

"Oh course, dear." She gave me another knowing smile.

I approached Jesse, allowing him to spoon sauce into my mouth. It was delectable, tangy and savory with a perfect hint of spice that left a lingering, pleasant sensation on my tongue.

Out of the corner of my eye, I noticed Max watching us from the front desk. Did he look amused? Or annoyed?

I looked at my watch. Shoot. My shift was about to start. That was probably why Max was looking at me. With a quick reassurance to Jesse about the sauce being just right, I hurriedly made my exit to start my shift.

Jesse looked a little disappointed but grinned and said he'd save me a plate for lunch.

"I'll be here," I called back.

At the front desk, Max gave me a rundown of the day's reservations and tasks. His tone was all business as usual, but I couldn't help feeling a twinge of...something towards him. Behind his laser focus and drive, there was a subtle vulnerability that shone through at times. I found myself wanting to know more about him.

He asked, "Can you also come by the office

when it's less busy? I still haven't quite figured out Excel and I know you're good at it."

My heart raced as I nodded eagerly. I didn't know why. What was so exciting about Excel?

"Sure. I can give you some tips."

But sometimes just standing next to Max gave me goosebumps.

Maybe I did have a type. I liked men with a bit of mysterious. Stella may be onto something.

About the Author

Harper Lin is a 3x *USA TODAY* bestselling cozy mystery author. When she's not reading or writing mysteries, she loves going to yoga classes, hiking, and baking with her family and friends.

For a complete list of her books by series, visit her website. www.HarperLin.com

Printed in Great Britain
by Amazon